THIS DIARY BELONGS TO:

Nikki J. Maxwell

PRIVATE & CONFIDENTIAL

If found, please return to ME for REWARD!

(NO SNOOPING ALLOWED!! ☹)

ALSO BY

Rachel Renée Russell

Dork Diaries

Rachel Renée Russell

DORK
diaries
Party Time

SIMON AND SCHUSTER

First published in Great Britain in 2010 by Simon and Schuster UK Ltd, a CBS company.

First published in the USA in 2010 by Aladdin, an imprint of Simon & Schuster Children's

Publishing Division.

Copyright © 2010 Rachel Renée Russell

Designed by Lisa Vega

The right of Rachel Renée Russell to be identified as the author and illustrator of this work

has been asserted by her in accordance with sections 77 and 78 of the Copyright, Design and

Patents Act, 1988.

Simon & Schuster UK Ltd

1st Floor, 222 Gray's Inn Road, London WC1X 8HB

A CIP catalogue record for this book is available from the British Library.

ISBN 978-0-85707-476-8

7 9 10 8 6

Printed and bound by CPI Group (UK) Ltd, Croydon, CRO 4YY

www.simonandschuster.co.uk

www.dorkdiaries.com

To my mom, Doris,
for ALWAYS being there for me

ACKNOWLEDGMENTS

To all my wonderful Dork Diaries fans — a special thank you for embracing this series so warmly and widely. Always remember to let your inner Dork shine through ☺!

Liesa Abrams, my awesome editor, thank you for the endless amounts of enthusiasm and energy you've brought to the Dork Diaries books. I am SO happy to be on this fabulous journey with you and your inner thirteen-year-old!

Lisa Vega, my superdedicated art director, thank you for your hard work and creative expertise. Especially on those long, late nights when the janitor had turned off all the lights.

Mara Anastas, Bethany Buck, Bess Braswell, Paul Crichton and the rest of my fantastic team at Aladdin/Simon & Schuster, thank you for believing in Dork Diaries.

Daniel Lazar, my incredible agent at Writers House,

thank you for being all that you are: agent, friend, adviser, coach, cheerleader and even therapist. You've helped make my wildest dreams come true. Also, a special thanks to Stephen Barr for sending me those crazy e-mails that made me laugh so hard I cried.

Maja Nikolic, Cecilia de la Campa, and Angharad Kowal, my foreign rights agents at Writers House, thank you for helping Dork Diaries be read internationally.

Nikki Russell, my daughter and supertalented assistant artist, thank you for all your hard work on this project. I could not have done any of this without you and cannot begin to express my gratitude. I am SO lucky to be your mom!

Sydney James, Cori James, Ariana Robinson, and Mikayla Robinson, my tweenage nieces, thank you for being my brutally honest critique partners who somehow know what's supercool before it actually is.

I can't believe this is happening to me!

I'm in the girls' bathroom FREAKING OUT!!

There's NO WAY I'm going to survive middle school.

I've just made a complete FOOL of myself in front of my secret crush. AGAIN ☹!!

And if that wasn't bad enough, I'm still stuck with a locker right next to MacKenzie Hollister's ☹!

Who, BTW, is the most popular girl at Westchester Country Day Middle School and a total SNOB. Calling her a "mean girl" is an understatement.

She's a KILLER SHARK in sparkly nail polish, designer jeans and platform Skechers.

But for some reason, everyone ADORES her.

MacKenzie and I do NOT get along. I'm guessing it's probably due to the fact that she

HATES MY GUTS ☹!!

She is forever gossiping behind my back and saying supermean stuff like that I have no fashion sense whatsoever and that our school mascot, Larry the Lizard, wears cuter clothes than I do.

Which might actually be true. But STILL!

I do NOT appreciate that girl BLABBING about my personal business.

This morning she was even more vicious than usual.

OMG, NIKKI!! Could you please go write in that diary somewhere else?! Your hideous green shirt is clashing with my new lip gloss flavour and it's giving me a MIGRAINE!

ME

I could NOT believe she actually said that to me!

I mean, how can a COLOUR clash with a FLAVOUR?!
DUH!! They're, like, two TOTALLY different,
um. . . THINGS!

That's when I lost it and yelled, "Sorry, MacKenzie!
But I'm REALLY busy right now. Can I IGNORE you
some other time?!"

But I just said it inside my head, so no one else
heard it but me.

And if all of that isn't enough TORTURE, the
annual WCD Halloween dance is in three weeks!

It's the biggest event of the fall, and everyone is
already gossiping about who's going with who.

I'd just totally DIE if my secret crush

asked me to go!

Yesterday he actually asked ME to be his lab partner for biology class!

I was SO excited, I did my Snoopy "happy dance".

La, La, La!
I'M . . .

La, La, La!
SO . . .

La, La, La!
HAPPY!!

And today I had a sneaking suspicion Brandon was going to "pop the question" about the Halloween dance.

The school day seemed to drag on FOREVER.

By the time I got to biology class, I was a nervous wreck.

Suddenly, a very troubling question popped into my head and I started to panic: what if Brandon only thought of me as a lab partner and nothing more?!

That's when I decided to try to impress him with my charm, wit and intelligence.

I gave him a big smile and went right to work drawing all these teeny-tiny lint-looking thingies I saw under the microscope.

Out of the corner of my eye, I could see Brandon staring at me with this urgent, yet very perplexed, look on his face.

It was obvious he wanted to talk to me about something SUPERserious. . . ☺!

Those thingies in the microscope really WERE just LINT! OMG!! I was SO EMBARRASSED!!

I knew right then and there I had pretty much blown any chance of Brandon asking me to the dance.

But the good news was, I had made a startling scientific discovery about the biogenetics of my intelligence and even reduced it to a working formula.

MY IQ ≤

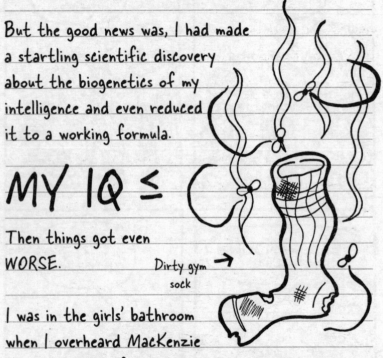

Then things got even WORSE.

Dirty gym sock →

I was in the girls' bathroom when I overheard MacKenzie bragging to her friends that she was practically almost 99.9% sure she and Brandon were going to the dance together as Edward and Bella from *Twilight*.

I was VERY disappointed, but not the least bit surprised. I mean, WHY would Brandon ask a total DORK like ME when he could go with a CCP (Cute, Cool & Popular) girl like MacKenzie?

And get this! As they were leaving, MacKenzie giggled and said she was buying a new lip gloss JUST for Brandon. I knew what THAT meant.

I was SO frustrated and angry at myself.

I waited until the bathroom was empty, and then I had a really good SCREAM.

ME →

AARGHH!!!

Which, for some strange reason, always makes me feel a lot better ☺.

Middle school can be very TRAUMATIZING, that's for sure!!

But the most important thing to remember is this: always remain CALM and try to handle your personal problems in a PRIVATE and MATURE manner.

ME, HAVING A PRIVATE SCREAM-FEST!

SATURDAY, OCTOBER 12

Today has been the MOST exciting day EVER!

I still can't believe I actually won first place and a $500 cash prize in our school's avant-garde art competition ☺!

Last week, without even telling me, Chloe, Zoey and Brandon entered photos of the tattoo designs I had drawn for kids at school.

So I totally freaked out when I found out I had won! Who would have thunk I'd beat out MacKenzie's awesome fashion illustrations?

And boy, was she ticked! Especially after bragging to everyone that she was going to win.

I can't wait to get my hands on all that money.

I had originally planned to use it to buy a mobile phone. But I decided it would be more prudent to save it for art camp next summer.

I'm investing in my dream of becoming an artist so I can spend all day curled up in bed in my fave pj's, drawing in my sketchbook and actually get paid for it. SWEET ☺!

Although, it would be kinda cool to use the money to fix up my very drab locker.

Adding a little bling would guarantee me a spot in the CCP clique.

ME, → showing off my awesome locker!

→ iPod stereo system

← colour TV + computer monitor combo

← VCR/DVD player

← personal ATM

ATM MACHINE

DVD

Anyway, practically the entire school was at the avant-garde art awards banquet today.

I was very shocked when MacKenzie came over and gave me a big hug.

I think she only did it to make a good impression, because what she said to me was not very sportsmanlike at all.

"Nikki! Congratulations on winning first place, hon! If I had known the art show judges wanted talentless junk, I would have framed my poodle's vomit stains and entered it as abstract art."

OMG! I couldn't believe she said that right to my face.

She should have just scribbled

"I'M SO JEALOUS!!"

across her forehead with a black marker. That probably would have been LESS obvious.

I was like, "Thanks, MacKenzie. You're such a big BABY. So cry me a river, build yourself a bridge and GET OVER IT!"

But I just said it inside my head, so no one else heard it but me. Mainly because I'm basically a nice person and I don't like negative vibes.

It had absolutely nothing to do with me being a little intimidated by her or anything.

Chloe and Zoey sat right next to me during dinner.

And as usual, we were acting really silly and having random giggle attacks.

When Brandon came over to take a picture of me for the school newspaper and yearbook, I thought I was going to DIE!

He suggested that we go to the atrium across the hall, where the lighting was better.

At first I was happy that Chloe and Zoey wanted to tag along, because I was supernervous.

But the entire time he was snapping pictures, they

were standing right behind him making kissy faces at me and acting all lovesick.

OMG! It was SO EMBARRASSING!!

I was so angry I wanted to grab them both by their necks and squeeze until their little heads exploded.

But instead, I just gritted my teeth and prayed
Brandon didn't notice them goofing around behind
his back like that.

Chloe and Zoey are really nice and sweet friends,
but sometimes I feel more like their babysitter than
their BFF.

Lucky for me, when they heard that dessert was
being served, they rushed back to the banquet to pig
out some more.

Which meant Brandon and I were all alone!

Only it was kind of uncomfortable and a little embarrassing because instead of talking, we just stared at each other and then the floor and then each other and then the floor and then each other and then the floor.

And this went on for what seemed like FOREVER!!

Then FINALLY he brushed his shaggy bangs out of his eyes and smiled at me kind of shylike. "I told you you were going to win. Congratulations!"

I gazed into his eyes, and my heart started to pound so loudly my toes were actually vibrating. Kind of like standing near a car blasting your favourite song, but with the windows rolled up. And you can't really hear the melody part, but your innermost soul can feel the vibrations from the bass part going *Thumpity-thump!! Thumpity-thump!!*

And my stomach felt all fluttery, like it was being

attacked by a huge swarm of very. . . ferocious. . . yet fragile. . . butterflies.

I immediately realised I was suffering from a relapse of RCS (Roller-Coaster Syndrome).

I clenched my teeth and mustered every ounce of strength in my entire body to keep myself from gleefully shouting, WHEEEEEEEEEEEEEEEE!!

But instead, I uttered something far, far worse.

"Thanks, Brandon. Um. . . have you tried those cute little barbecued

wing—dings? They're actually quite delicious!"

"Did you just say. . . wing—dings?!"

"Yep. They're at the front table right near the punch. They also have honey glazed and hot-'n'-spicy. But the barbecued ones are my favourite."

"Um. . . actually, no! I haven't tried them."

"Well, you really should. . ."

"So, I. . . um. . . want to ask you something. . ."

"About the wing—dings?"

Brandon's face was intensely serious.

"No. Actually, I want to know if. . . you. . ."

I was holding my breath and hanging on to his every word.

". . . I mean, it would be totally cool if you would—"

"BRANDON!! There you are!! OMG! I've been looking for you everywhere!"

MacKenzie barged into the room and lunged straight for Brandon like an NFL linebacker trying to recover a fumbled ball.

"As the official school photographer, you really need to get a picture of me posing with my Fab-4-Ever fashion illustrations. They're about to take down my display!"

Then she just stood there smiling at Brandon all GOOGLY-EYED, twirling her hair around her finger.

Which was obviously a DESPERATE attempt to HYPNOTIZE him into doing her EVIL bidding.

"Brandon, please hurry! Before it's too late!" she whined breathlessly while glaring at me in total disgust like I was this huge pimple that had suddenly popped out on her nose or something.

Brandon rolled his eyes, sighed and gave me this very goofy but cute smile.

"So. . . we'll talk later, Nikki. Okay?"

"Sure. See ya."

As I walked back to the awards banquet, I felt very light-headed and a little nauseous.

But in a really GOOD way!

More than anything, I was now totally consumed with a burning curiosity.

Brandon had been about to ask me something really important when MacKenzie had rudely interrupted him.

Which left me with one very obvious and compelling question:

WHY AM I SUCH AN IDIOT?!!

Wing–dings?! I could NOT believe I had rambled on and on about the variety of delicious wing–ding flavours!

No wonder he didn't ask me to the dance.

At least my picture came out okay.

Brandon is such an AWESOME photographer!

I'm in the most HORRIBLE mood right now! I'm SO totally dreading school tomorrow.

If I hear one more girl mention that stupid dance, I'm going to SCREAM!! I keep hoping someone will ask me, but I know it's NOT going to happen.

What I need is a MAGIC love potion or something!

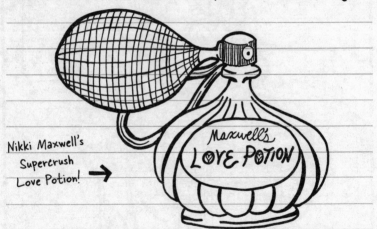

Nikki Maxwell's Supercrush Love Potion! →

Maxwell's LOVE POTION

I would definitely use it on Brandon because that's the ONLY way he'd ever like a LOSER like me.

Then I'd share it with girls all over the world who are suffering from the same problem.

Just one spray and your crush will fall madly in love with the first person he lays eyes on!

SUPERCRUSH LOVE POTION!
NOW EVERY GIRL CAN LIVE HAPPILY EVER
AFTER WITH THE GUY OF HER DREAMS!

Or maybe... NOT!!

Okay, so maybe my love potion idea is really

STUPID!!

My life is HOPELESS!! ☹!!

Tonight Mom and my little sister, Brianna, were putting up decorations for Halloween.

I knew what was coming next because it happens every single year.

Brianna sneaks up on everyone and tries to scare us with this big stupid-looking plastic spider.

It's almost like a Maxwell family Halloween tradition or something. Mom and Dad always put on this big act and pretend to be superscared just to humour her. And, of course, Brianna gets a really big kick out of it.

Personally, I don't think it's healthy to encourage her like that. What's going to happen when she gets older and starts attending middle school?

Hey! I already KNOW what's going to happen!

Brianna's going to take that plastic spider to school and shake it at people because she thinks it's appropriate behaviour.

And everyone at her school will think she's NUTZ!

Then I'll have to go through all the trouble of changing my last name so no one will know she's my sister.

My parents need to realise that raising an impressionable child like Brianna is a big responsibility.

Anyway, I was up in my room studying for my French test.

I was feeling a little grumpy because I was having a hard time remembering which nouns in French are masculine versus feminine.

Sure enough, Brianna showed up just like I expected:

I TOTALLY FREAKED!!

And that poor spider seemed a little traumatised too.

Brianna thought the whole thing was SO funny.

HA HA HA, Brianna!!

I don't know HOW I thought that real spider was Brianna's fake one.

Hers is purple with little pink hearts on it and is wearing high top sneakers and a big cheesy smile. It looks like the type of spider you'd find living in a Barbie Dream House or hanging out with SpongeBob SquarePants.

After that experience, I'll never forget that "spider" in French is _araignée._

But, is it a masculine noun OR a feminine noun?!

OH, CRUD!!

I'm SO going to FLUNK this stupid test ☹!!

When I arrived at school this morning, I was surprised to see a note on my locker door from Chloe and Zoey:

NIKK!,

GUESS WHO'S GOING TO THE HALLOWEEN DANCE?! MEET US IN

THE JANITOR'S CLOSET ASAP!!

☺ CHLOE + ZOEY

The janitor's closet is our secret hangout.

We meet there to discuss very important PRIVATE and HIGHLY CONFIDENTIAL personal stuff.

As soon as I stepped inside, I could tell Chloe and Zoey were superexcited.

"Guess who's going to the Halloween dance?!!" Zoey giggled happily.

"Um. . . I dunno. WHO?" I asked.

I was pretty darn sure it WASN'T one of us. We were the three biggest dorks in the entire school.

"SURPRISE!! WE ARE!!" Chloe screamed, jumping up and down and giving me jazz hands.

"And we've already arranged for three guys to be our dates! Sort of!" Zoey squealed.

"Sort of? What do you mean by 'sort of'?" I asked.

I was already starting to get a really bad feeling about this guy thing.

That's when Chloe and Zoey explained their crazy

plan for how we were going to snag really cool dates for the Halloween dance.

All in just five easy steps:

STEP 1: We sign up to be volunteers for the Halloween dance clean-up crew.

STEP 2: We arrive at the dance half an hour early, pretending like we're there to inspect for cleanliness. But instead, we secretly change into our fabulous costumes.

STEP 3: We quickly spread the rumour that the three cutest guys onstage with the band are our dates (even though they're really NOT).

STEP 4: Since the band is going to be busy performing the ENTIRE night, the three of us will dance, eat and hang out with one another.

STEP 5: We'll have FUN, FUN, FUN while everyone (including the CCPs) RAVES about our SUPERcute, SUPERtalented, SUPER-pop-star dates.

This plan was *ALMOST* as bizarre as the one where they were going to run away and live in the secret underground tunnels of the New York City Public Library.

I told them there was a slight chance their phony "My date's a band member!" scheme might work.

But it would mostly depend on what the guys in the band actually looked like.

CUTE 'N' MOODY MUSIC LOVERS . . .

Everyone would ENVY us ☺!

Everyone would LAUGH at us ☹!

The dangerous part is that this whole thing could easily backfire and ruin our reputations.

And the three of us already have a pretty pathetic ranking in the WCD CCP Popularity Index.

Here is a chart of the most UNPOPULAR people in our entire school.

NINE MOST <u>UNPOPULAR</u>

ME

1 2 3 4 5 6 7 8 9

1. Violet Baker
2. Theodore L. Swagmire III
3. Zoey Franklin
4. Janitor
5. Chloe Garcia
6. Head Lunch Lady
7. Larry the Lizard (school mascot)
8. Nikki Maxwell
9. Black Slime Mold (growing in locker room shower)

Since there would be a substantial risk I could end up more UNPOPULAR than black slime mold, we definitely needed to come up with a way better idea.

I suggested that we each make an inexpensive yet creative costume by taking a big green rubbish bag and stuffing it full of newspaper and going as. . . (drumroll please). . .

BAGS OF RUBBISH!!

How CUTE would that be?!

Especially if we were members of the clean-up crew.

We'd also need a pair of those yellow rubber gloves.

Just thinking about all the germy things that could be lying around after a big party like that actually made me shudder.

Ewwww!

And since we didn't have dates, we could spend the entire night doing Broadway-style dance numbers using a broom, mop and vacuum cleaner as our dance partners.

I personally thought my plan was pure GENIUS!

Us rocking it at the dance as. . .

THE CLEANING CREW!

But Chloe and Zoey were like, "Um. . . no offence, Nikki, but your idea is actually kind of. . . LAME."

Of course that little comment really ticked me off.

"Okay, girlfriends! You wanna know what I think is LAME?! LAME is attending the Halloween dance as the clean-up crew and then LYING to everyone that the band members are our dates!"

Chloe and Zoey got really quiet and just stood there staring at me with these big sad puppy-dog eyes.

And of course I felt kind of sorry for them because I personally knew what it was like to very desperately want to attend the dance.

So, being the sensitive and caring friend that I am, I decided to put aside my personal feelings and sign up for the Halloween dance clean-up crew.

I considered it a small sacrifice that would ultimately nurture true and lasting friendships.

The sign-up sheets for the Halloween dance committees were posted on the bulletin board right outside the office door.

Luckily for us, no one had signed up for the clean-up crew yet.

The thing that really bothered me though was the sign-up sheet for CHAIRPERSON of the Halloween dance committees.

SIGN-UP SHEET
HALLOWEEN DANCE
CHAIRPERSON*

~~Ryan Crenshaw~~
~~Brianne Wane~~
~~Christina Hughes~~
~~Paige Clark~~
Violet Baker
THEODORE L. SWAGMIRE III
MacKenzie Hollister

*TO BE SELECTED BY STUDENT COUNCIL

For some reason, most of the people who had signed up had crossed their names off the list.

Which meant there were only three candidates for that position ☹!

PLEASE, PLEASE, PLEASE

let Violet Baker or Theodore L. Swagmire III be selected as chairperson.

Otherwise, this clean-up crew thing was going to turn into my worst

NIGHTMARE!

TUESDAY, OCTOBER 15

I LOVE fifth hour because Chloe, Zoey and I get to work as library shelving assistants (LSAs) ☺!

Some kids think the library is a quiet and boring place where only dorks and nerds hang out, but we always have a BLAST!

WE PUT BOOKS BACK ON THE SHELVES.

And our librarian, Mrs Peach, is supernice. On Fridays she bakes us these humongous double chocolate chip cookies with walnuts. Yummy!

I was a little surprised when Mrs Peach gave me a note saying I was supposed to report to the office immediately.

My parents were there waiting for me. They were picking me up from school early because they wanted me to attend the funeral of a Mr Wilbur Roach, a local retired businessman and former president of the Westchester Exterminators Association.

I couldn't believe that was actually his REAL name! Poor guy!

My parents and I had never met him. But since exterminators from all over the state were going to be there with their families, Dad thought it might be a good idea if we attended too.

I was like, JUST GREAT ☹!! And as if that wasn't bad enough, I had to listen to Dad's

47

Pure Disco 3 CD the whole drive there and back.

By the time I'd heard the song "Shake Your Groove Thing" for the thirty-ninth consecutive time, I wanted to jump out of the car window into oncoming traffic.

It goes, "Shake your groove thing, shake your groove thing, yeah, yeah," and then you just repeat those words 1,962 times until the song is over.

The whole experience ended up being very traumatic for me. I was also upset because I had a bad case of hiccups. Extremely loud ones.

During the memorial service, Mom kept giving me this dirty look like I was hiccupping on purpose or something. But I honestly couldn't help it.

And this guy named Mr Hubert Dinkle got really choked up while he was up there giving the eulogy. Mom said it was because Wilbur Roach was his best friend.

I think my hiccups must have got on his nerves or something because he stopped right in the middle of his speech, gave me the evil eye and growled.

I am so NOT lying. He actually growled at me!

My hiccups were driving everyone nuts.

I was waiting for Wilbur Roach to sit up and YELL at me too!

Although, THAT would have totally freaked me out! Mainly because he was supposed to be, like, you know. . . DEAD!!!!

Anyway, my hiccups kept getting worse. Then Mr Dinkle got an attitude and acted pretty RUDE about the whole thing.

After Mr Dinkle practically SCARED me to death AND made me drink that big glass of water in front of everyone, my hiccups *finally* stopped! Which was a good thing ☺!

I always wondered why they kept a pitcher of water up there next to the podium like that.

Who would have thunk it was for an emergency cure for a case of hiccups?!

After all the drama at that funeral, I'm pretty sure Mom and Dad won't be dragging me to another one anytime soon.

Thank goodness for that!

My only worry now is that since Mr Dinkle is superold and a part-time church organist, I might unexpectedly run into him again at some point in the future.

And then he'll give me a REALLY hard time for ruining his speech.

MR DINKLE'S REVENGE

53

OMG!

I have NEVER laughed so hard in my entire life!

My mom got up extra early this morning and tried out some homemade beauty treatments and relaxation techniques that she'd seen on television.

She was wearing an oatmeal face mask with cucumbers on her eyes. And she had turned off all the lights in the family room to meditate on the meaning of her life.

That's what she said she was doing, anyway. Although, it looked to me like she was sitting in the chair snoozing.

Anyway, Dad walked in and turned on the lights and like

TOTALLY FREAKED!

His scream was so loud and high-pitched, I thought it was going to shatter that big window in our family room.

Then, when Mom woke up and heard Dad screaming like that, she totally panicked and grabbed hold of him.

Which made him scream even LOUDER!

I guess Dad must have thought he was being attacked by some kind of oatmeal-crusted, cucumber-eyed zombie wearing a pink fuzzy robe with a bath towel wrapped around its head.

Which, I have to admit, DOES sound awfully scary when you think about it.

I only wish I could have caught that moment on video. I bet it would have got, like, 10 million views on YouTube.

Then some producer would have paid us a million dollars to do our own cheesy reality show.

OMG! I'm still laughing so hard my stomach hurts!

☺!!!

BTW, I have a really bad feeling about Chloe, Zoey and me being on that clean-up crew.

WHY?

Because when I got to school, everyone was buzzing about the student council selecting MACKENZIE to be the chairperson of our Halloween dance!

JUST CRAPTASTIC ☹!!

Of course she made a big fat hairy deal out of the whole thing.

She actually wore a special outfit for the occasion and insisted that everyone address her as "Miss Chairperson."

I personally thought the tiara and roses were a bit much.

It's not like I was jealous of her or anything.

Like, how juvenile would that be?

The first thing MacKenzie did was call an emergency meeting during lunch.

Only, there wasn't any type of REAL emergency that I could see.

Thirty of us just sat there in this huge auditorium listening to her make a ridiculous speech:

"I just wanted to congratulate my wonderful Halloween dance committee members and share with all of you my extraordinary vision for what will be the most spectacular event our school has ever experienced. In keeping with this goal, I am officially inviting each and every one of you to my very own birthday party. Which, BTW, has been rescheduled again for Saturday, October nineteenth, due to a conflict with the art awards banquet. I proudly extend this opportunity in hopes that a few of you more, um. . . shall we say. . . socially challenged individuals might experience firsthand what a glamourous and exciting party is like."

I almost fell out of my seat!

I could not believe MacKenzie had just called me
socially challenged right in front of everyone, AND
invited me to her BIRTHDAY PARTY!!!

Like, WHY would she want ME at her party?!

MacKenzie's speech went on for another ten
minutes and when she finally finished, all the CCPs
gave her a standing ovation.

MacKenzie said the committees for set-up,
entertainment, publicity, decorations and food would
meet daily starting tomorrow.

But the clean-up crew — which, BTW, was me, Chloe,
Zoey, Violet Baker and Theodore L. Swagmire III —
didn't need any meetings "because it doesn't take a
brain to clean up."

It was very obvious to me that MacKenzie was
treating us clean-up crew members like second-class
citizens and I didn't like it one bit.

I personally felt it was of vital importance that we meet at least once to plan our cleaning strategy.

Next she encouraged everyone to come up with really creative Halloween costumes.

EXCEPT, of course, the clean-up crew. MacKenzie showed everyone sketches of the "supercute" uniform she had personally designed for us to wear the entire night.

OUR CLEAN-UP CREW OUTFITS DESIGNED BY MACKENZIE

It looked like a twist between a spacesuit and flannel underwear and came with four-inch platform boots.

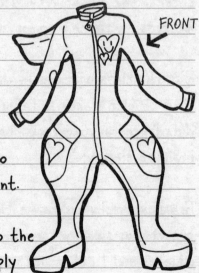

FRONT

She said we could easily store twenty kilos of trash in each of the two large pockets in the front.

And if we had to go to the bathroom, we could simply

unbutton the large flap in
the back.

BACK

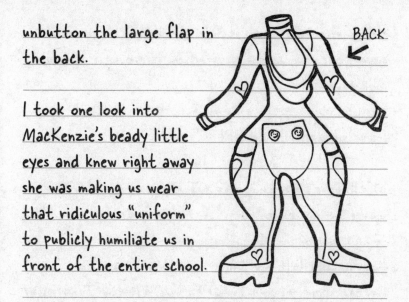

I took one look into
MacKenzie's beady little
eyes and knew right away
she was making us wear
that ridiculous "uniform"
to publicly humiliate us in
front of the entire school.

But she just smiled and batted her eyelashes all
innocent like.

After the meeting was finally over, I told Chloe
and Zoey there was NO WAY IN HECK I was going
to allow that girl to embarrass us like that.

But they were so excited about the possibility of
going to the dance that they didn't even care.

They told me I should try a little harder to be
more of a team player and give MacKenzie's uniform
a chance.

Because, even though it was absolutely hideous on paper, once we actually tried on the outfit it might look supercute.

I was so mad I could SPIT!

MacKenzie's meeting was a TOTAL and MASSIVE waste of my time.

I personally felt my lunch hour would have been better spent trying to KEEP DOWN the Tuna Fish/ Meat Loaf Casserole Leftover Surprise!

Brianna had a ballet recital this evening. I wanted to stay home and do my homework, but Mom said I had to go.

Every year it's exactly the same thing: cutesy little girls dressed up in cutesy little costumes, doing cutesy little dance routines to cutesy little songs.

Brianna didn't want to go to the recital either.

Mainly because she HATED ballet!!

Whenever Mom dragged her off to lessons, she would whine, "Moooommm! I wanna be a karate-chop girl! Not one of those pointy-toe-hoppers with the pink scratchy skirts!"

But since Mom had dreamed of taking ballet lessons when she was a little girl, she felt the next best thing was to give birth to a daughter and force HER to do it instead!

When I was younger, Mom tried to enroll me in a ballet class too.

Only after she dropped me off, I went straight to the girls' bathroom and ditched my leotard and ballet flats and changed into more appropriate dance attire. The COOL kind they wear on MTV.

Even though I was superexcited about dancing, my ballet teacher sent me home with a note:

Madame FuFu's
School of Dance

WE TURN CLUMSY, UGLY DUCKLINGS INTO
BEAUTIFUL, GRACEFUL SWANS.

Dear _Mrs Maxwell_ :

I have carefully evaluated the dance skills of

your daughter, _Nikki_ , and I suggest the

following placement:

_____ BEGINNING BALLET CLASS

_____ BEGINNING JAZZ CLASS

_____ BEGINNING TAP CLASS

__X__ OTHER: _Professional backup_

dancer for pop star or rapper.

Good luck!

Sincerely,

Madame FuFu

Madame FuFu

I thought this was great news, but mom was pretty
much heartbroken I wasn't going to be a ballerina.

65

Unfortunately, Madame FuFu didn't like Brianna all that much either.

She was always sending her home early for disrupting the dance class.

And just last week Brianna got in trouble for defacing ballet school property.

Instead of simply apologising to Madame FuFu, Brianna lied about the whole thing.

She was like, "But, Mommy! My friend Miss Penelope wrote on that stupid ballet poster! Not ME!"

That was her story and she was sticking to it.

But everyone knows Miss Penelope is actually Brianna's OWN hand with a face doodled on it.

Everyone except Brianna.

It's quite obvious to me my kid sister has some serious mental issues. I'm just sayin'. . . !!

Overall, the recital went okay. Except for the last dance number, called "Fairies and Flower Friends Have Fabulous Fun."

Brianna just stood there on the stage shivering, with this terrified look on her face. I felt kind of sorry for her.

Brianna

Although, I have to admit, it was partly my fault.

Brianna has this thing about the tooth fairy. She's been scared to death of her ever since I told her the tooth fairy took teeth from little children and Super Glued them together to make dentures for old people.

THE TOOTH FAIRY GLUING TEETH TO MAKE DENTURES

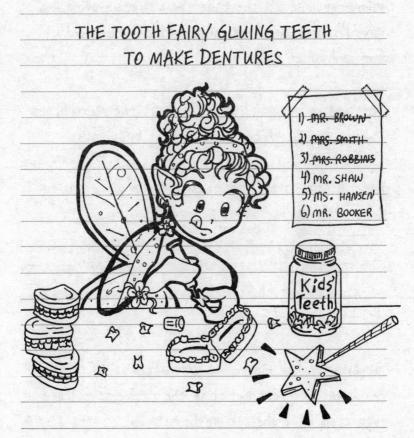

1) ~~MR. BROWN~~
2) ~~MRS. SMITH~~
3) ~~MRS. ROBBINS~~
4) MR. SHAW
5) MS. HANSEN
6) MR. BOOKER

Kids' Teeth

I totally meant it as just an innocent little joke.

But now she's too afraid to go to the bathroom by herself at night.

Anyway, after the recital was over, we were getting ready to leave when Mrs Clarissa Hargrove, one of the ballet moms, came over and gave Brianna an invitation to a Halloween party for the ballet class.

She said it was going to be held at the Westchester Zoo in the Children's Petting Zoo building.

I was a little surprised when Mrs Hargrove congratulated me on my art award.

She said she was desperately looking for an artist to paint faces for the ballet party and was wondering if I would be interested.

Apparently, her niece, who also attends WCD, told her I was the best artist in the entire school and suggested that she ask me to help out.

And GET THIS!

Mrs Hargrove offered me $150 to paint faces and
help with games for a couple of hours.

I was like, "Well, um. . . HECK YEAH!! ☺!!"

For $150, I would have painted her ENTIRE house.
Inside and out!

It's not like I was going to be doing anything
important on Halloween night anyway.

Except maybe cleaning up after the Halloween dance.

And now I had a really good excuse for NOT doing
that phony "My date's a band member!" thing with
Chloe and Zoey.

Mrs Hargrove said she would buy the paint and
brushes and drop everything off next week.

So now I'm sitting in my room staring at a cheque
for $150.

I can't believe I FINALLY have the money to get that phone I've been wanting.

I'm still obsessing over what Brandon wanted to ask me that night at the awards banquet.

According to MacKenzie (and all the latest gossip), he already has a date for the Halloween dance.

So the only other thing I can think of is that maybe he still wants to interview me about winning the art show since he asked me about it nine days ago.

Whenever I see him in class, he just says hi and bye and that's pretty much it. He's definitely a lot quieter than he used to be.

Or maybe he just doesn't want to be seen in public talking to a big DORK like me ☹!

MacKenzie doesn't help things either. Every time she sees Brandon and me near each other, she rushes over and tries to flirt with him by twirling her hair. She's been doing this ALL week. I definitely think she's up to something, but I don't know what.

I finally mentioned the whole Brandon thing to Chloe and Zoey while we were putting away books.

Chloe, who, BTW, is an expert on guy stuff, said I should simply ask him what he wanted.

I told her I had already tried to do that. But it was really difficult to talk to him during class with MacKenzie always butting in.

And if I asked him to meet me in the janitor's closet for a little privacy, he would think I was a WEIRDO.

Chloe and Zoey agreed with me 100%. Not about it being hard to talk to Brandon during class, but about him thinking I was a weirdo.

Then Zoey said she had overheard MacKenzie bragging in gym class that the editor of the school newspaper had assigned Brandon to cover her birthday party as a personal favour.

That's when Chloe said, "Hey, I have an idea! If

Brandon is going to be at MacKenzie's party, why don't you just talk to him there? It'll only take a few minutes and then you can leave."

"Are you KA-RAY-ZEE?!" I screamed. "There is no way in HECK I'm going to a party by myself with MacKenzie and all those CCPs!!"

That's when Chloe got this big sly grin on her face and started doing jazz hands!

I was like, UH-OH!! Not another of her WACKY ideas?!!

"Nikki, you're not going there ALONE! Because WE'RE coming with you!" Chloe shouted excitedly.

I could NOT believe Chloe and Zoey both volunteered to go with me to MacKenzie's party!

They said it was for moral support and because they're my BFFs.

And NOT because they wanted to have fun, dance,

or flirt with their secret crushes, Jason and Ryan, who, BTW, might ask them to the Halloween dance.

NOPE! We all agreed that MacKenzie's party was going to be strictly BUSINESS!

I had originally planned to use the $150 cheque from Mrs Hargrove to buy a new phone.

But when I checked my clothes, the only superfancy party dress I owned was from second grade and had buttons and bows all over it.

And I wouldn't be caught dead wearing that plain old dress from the awards banquet.

So I decided to use my phone money to buy a glamourous, designer, semiformal dress to wear to MacKenzie's party.

And for once my mom actually agreed to take me to the MALL instead of our usual discount department stores!!

I was like, YES ☺!!

While Mom helped Brianna shop for a Halloween costume, I went from store to store trying on the most fabulous dresses. I even found shoes, jewellery and other cool stuff to match each one.

I actually felt like I was doing a photo shoot for *America's Next Top Model!* All I needed was for Tyra Banks to suddenly appear.

She'd smile at me and another model very warmly and say, "I hold two photos in my hand. But only

ONE of you can continue in this competition. The ugly, lazy girl gotta pack and go home, y'all."

OMG! I just LOVE that girl ☺! I think she's a wonderful role model for teens.

Anyway, I had a BLAST trying on all those clothes!

WACKO
EMO

DRAMA
QUEEN
MEAN

BAGGY
SHABBY
CHIC

RAGING
REBEL
ROCKER

GOTH
GIRL
GROOVY

VERY
SCARY
VAMPY

79

COS GIRL CUTIE →

← SILLY CELEBUTANT

Unfortunately, none of these styles reflected the real and true me.

The mall was going to close in less than an hour and I was starting to panic. If I didn't find a dress, I couldn't go to MacKenzie's party.

Suddenly . . .

THERE IT WAS!!

But the only dress in my size was on this very
snotty-looking mannequin in the window.

So I rushed over to this very snobby-looking sales
clerk and tapped her on the shoulder and said,

"Excuse me, ma'am. But I absolutely LOVE that dress in the window! Could you please take it off the mannequin?"

But she was very busy putting out a very colourful display of toe socks.

And I'm guessing she did NOT want to be disturbed, because she just glared at me and said, "Young lady, can't you see I'm busy? Now SHOO! Before I call security!"

I was totally shocked by her totally inappropriate behaviour!

I even considered lodging a complaint with the manager since this was supposed to be an exclusive store for upscale customers.

Like, WHO in their right mind would even want to buy a pair of toe socks?!

I'm just saying. . .

Anyway, I really, really LOVED that dress!

And there was no way I was leaving that store without it.

So I decided to sneak inside the window display and take the dress off that mannequin myself.

I mean, how hard could it be?

Lucky for me, the only other person around was a little old lady browsing the support tights.

Things were going really well until I accidentally knocked her over and her head popped right off.

Not the little old lady's head, the mannequin's.

I was like, "Oh, CRUD!"

Every time I tried to stand her up, she would just teeter back and forth and fall right over again. And her head would roll across the floor like a bowling ball.

To make matters worse, a crowd of people had gathered around the window and were staring at me.

And this toddler was crying really loud because that headless mannequin must have looked pretty dang scary.

Anyway, after what seemed like forever, I finally got that mannequin to stand up. I also found a new outfit for her to wear.

Then I paid for the dress and got the heck out of there.

Before that mean sales clerk called security and had me arrested me for vandalising the window display.

Believe me, I WON'T be shopping at that swanky department store anytime soon.

SATURDAY, OCTOBER 19

OMG! I can't believe what just happened to me at MacKenzie's party. I have never been so humiliated in my entire life ☹!

Her party was at a ritzy country club and looked like something straight out of that MTV show *My Super Sweet 16.*

A humongous room had been converted into a dance club, complete with a stage, a DJ and strobe lights.

And to really make things upscale, a private chef was preparing sushi and freshly baked pizza while a Starbucks barista served mocha Frappucinos, caramel lattes and strawberry-banana Vivanno smoothies.

All the guys were decked out in suits and ties and the girls were wearing party dresses by all the most famous designers.

There must have been two hundred kids there, and everyone was dancing and having fun.

I was like, WOW!!

Chloe and Zoey looked FANTASTIC! And they said I looked like a glamourous Hollywood celebutant.

The three of us felt supernervous and totally out of place being there with all those CCP kids.

We placed our presents for MacKenzie on an overflowing gift table and then tried to act coolly nonchalant.

You know, like we really WEREN'T dorks and it really WASN'T the first and ONLY middle school party we'd ever been invited to.

But Zoey kind of messed up our "very cool party girl" cover.

Suddenly her eyes widened to the size of golf balls and she let out a high-pitched "SQUEE!"

On a nearby table was this huge chocolate fountain.

It had a fancy crystal platter piled high with an assortment of fresh cut fruit for dipping into the warm chocolate.

The three of us practically ran over to take a closer look.

It was the most AWESOME thing ever!!

And while we were standing there, the strangest
thing happened.

Jason and Ryan walked right up to Chloe and Zoey
and asked them to dance!!!

The three of us just froze and went into total
shock.

I thought for sure we were going to need one of those defibrillator thingies that medics use when people have heart attacks.

Chloe and Zoey just stood there blinking, with their mouths dangling open, like deer caught in headlights or something.

They looked at me and then the guys, then back at me, then at the guys, then back at me and then at the guys again. This went on, like, forever!

Finally, I spoke up.

"Actually, they'd LOVE to dance!"

That's when Chloe and Zoey started blushing profusely.

"Um. . . sure!" Zoey squeaked.

"Okay, I guess!" Chloe giggled.

Then they both squeezed my arm. And because I'm their BFF, I knew just what they were thinking.

That maybe the guys were going to ask them to the Halloween dance.

I kind of winked and said, "Hey! Go right ahead! I'm going to try this yummy chocolate fountain. Have fun, 'kay?"

Chloe and Zoey smiled nervously as the four of them made their way to the crowded dance floor.

I was SO happy for them.

I couldn't make up my mind which fruit I wanted to try first – strawberry, apple, pineapple, banana or kiwi. However, since it was free, I just piled a few of each on my plate and then drizzled warm chocolate over the whole thing. I couldn't wait to dig in!

It was hard to believe I was actually enjoying myself at MacKenzie's party. If only I could find Brandon and *finally* get to talk to him about that interview or whatever, it would be a PERFECT night.

I was a little surprised when MacKenzie and her BFF, Jessica, walked up to me and started talking.

"OMG! I can't believe you actually came!" MacKenzie said, smiling at me. "And your dress and shoes are supercute! Wait, don't tell me. You raided lost and found?!"

I gritted my teeth, took a deep breath and then plastered a fake smile on my face.

"Happy birthday, MacKenzie! And thanks for inviting me!"

I didn't want to waste any of my energy dealing with her drama. The ONLY reason I had come to her stupid party was to talk to Brandon.

Suddenly Jessica stared at me and then scowled.

"OMG! What's that on your fruit? Eww!"

"What?!" I looked down at it, expecting to see
a bug or a hair or something stuck in the
chocolate.

"THAT! Don't you see it? GROSS!" she exclaimed,
pointing and frowning like she saw something slimy
with eighteen legs.

I brought my plate up for a closer look.

"What? I don't see any—"

But before I could finish my sentence, Jessica
slapped the bottom of my plate.

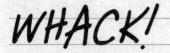

WHACK!

As the plate went airborne, a few stray pieces
of fruit landed in the chocolate fountain with a
kerplunk, splashing chocolate on my face.

However, the vast majority of the gooey mess landed on the front of my dress in chunks and stuck there.

I froze and stared at it all in HORROR!

My beautiful designer dress was totally ruined!

MacKenzie and Jessica doubled over in laughter and a half dozen other CCP girls joined in.

"I am SO sorry, Nikki! It was totally an accident!" Jessica sneered.

"OMG, Nikki! You should have seen the look on your face!!" MacKenzie shrieked.

"It looks like you were in a food fight. And LOST!" Jessica snorted.

The lump in my throat was so large I could barely breathe. Tears filled my eyes and I tried to blink them away. I didn't want to give MacKenzie and Jessica the pleasure of seeing me cry.

I grabbed some napkins and wiped my dress until all that remained was a large, faint brown stain.

It suddenly became very clear that the only reason MacKenzie had invited me to her party was to publicly humiliate me.

And, like an idiot, I had taken the bait. How could I have been so STUPID?! I didn't care about talking to Brandon anymore. I just wanted to go home.

Suddenly, MacKenzie gasped and whipped out her lip gloss. "OMG! Jess, isn't that the photographer from the Westchester Society Page? I think it's time for our close-up!"

That's when I noticed that the fountain was vibrating and making a strange gurgling sound.

I guessed that the pieces of fruit that had dropped inside were clogging things up or something.

"What a beautiful fountain! Let's get a shot with the birthday girl and her best friend standing right beside it," the photographer guy said as he dunked a huge strawberry into the chocolate and popped it into his mouth.

Okay, I had a really bad feeling about their taking a photo for the Westchester Society Page right next to that fountain.

Mainly because it was making a low rumbling noise that sounded like a twist between a clogged-up garbage disposal and a plugged-up toilet.

It was NOT a happy sound. I was outta there!

I admit, that big smudge on my dress looked bad.

But MacKenzie and Jessica looked like they'd been mud wrestling in a vat of chocolate fudge and then tried to clean up by showering in chocolate syrup.

Which, BTW, made me feel a whole lot better ☺.

I wrapped my shawl over my dress and then hurried to the front desk in the lobby to call my parents.

I decided not to tell Chloe and Zoey I was leaving.

They were still dancing with Jason and Ryan and seemed to be having a really great time.

And if they were lucky and landed "real" dates for the Halloween dance, they wouldn't have to do that phony "My date's a band member!" thing.

I was standing outside the main door, waiting for my parents and trying to ignore a really bad headache, when I heard a familiar voice.

"Hey, are you leaving already?"

It was Brandon. Just great ☹!!

I adjusted my shawl to make sure that stain wasn't showing and just stared straight ahead.

"Yeah, I am. Actually, I don't even know why I came."

"I'm outta here too. I just needed shots for the newspaper."

"Um. . . that's nice, I guess," I said, trying to muster a smile.

Our eyes met, but I quickly looked away. We both just stood there not saying anything.

I kept fiddling with my shawl, but out of the corner of my eye I could see him staring at me.

"Are you okay?"

"Yep. Just supertired."

"I'm sorry to hear that. . ."

"Oh! Here's my dad. See ya."

I rushed to the curb to meet the car as it pulled into the U-shaped driveway.

"Hey, wait a minute, Nikki! I just—"

Without looking back, I opened the car door and collapsed into the backseat.

I was exhausted, angry, humiliated and confused.

And to make matters worse, I think I was having my first migraine.

More than anything, I just didn't have the energy to chitchat with Brandon right then.

As my dad pulled away, I peeked into the rearview mirror.

Under the glare of the street light, I could see him just standing there in the middle of the street with his hands in his pockets and a hurt look on his face.

I suddenly felt like the most CRUEL and HEARTLESS person in the world.

I buried my head in my shawl

and had a really good cry right there in the backseat.

WHY was I acting so crazy?

WHY was everything so confusing?

WHY was I hurting a person I really cared about?

It was just another DREADFUL day in the PATHETIC life of a not-so-popular party girl ☹!

SUNDAY, OCTOBER 20

When I woke up this morning, I was in a decent mood.

For about thirty seconds.

Then all the HORRIBLE memories from MacKenzie's party came flooding into my brain like a massive tidal wave.

I just wanted to crawl deep under the covers and hide there for the rest of the school year.

ME

DO NOT DISTURB!

Now I'm feeling hopelessly depressed ☹.

I checked my answering machine and was not that surprised to see Chloe and Zoey had each left me, like, a dozen messages.

But I decided NOT to call them back. The last thing I felt like doing was blabbing on the phone for three hours about how MacKenzie and Jessica had tortured me and destroyed my dress.

Although, I can't blame Chloe and Zoey for being supermad at me for just disappearing into thin air like that.

I'd wanted to get the heck out of there as fast as possible. I guess I completely BUGGED OUT!

Anyway, around noon my mom came bouncing up the stairs to tell me that lunch was ready. Then out of the blue she smiled really big and said, "Guess what, honey?! I have a little surprise for you!"

ME, TRYING TO GUESS WHAT'S IN THE BOX

THIS SIDE UP

And NO. I DIDN'T think she had finally got me a mobile phone. Even though I've been wanting one, like, FOREVER!

Apparently, Dad was sorting through stuff in the attic when he discovered a box of Mom's old costumes from her Shakespeare theater days back in college.

When she showed me her Juliet costume, I was like, WOW!

The dress was made of the most beautiful plush purple velvet and had gold embroidered trim along the sleeves and skirt.

It came with a curly wig and a fancy eye mask decorated with purple beads, ribbons and feathers.

The outfit looked like something a real princess might wear. And it was in great condition, even after being in storage all those years.

Because the dress had a lace-up front, Mom thought it would fit me perfectly. She said I was welcome to use it for the Halloween dance.

I thanked her and told her it was the best costume ever.

But when she begged me to try it on, I kind of stammered and came up with the excuse that I had to study for a big test. I promised her I would try it on after dinner.

Which, BTW, was a lie. I absolutely LOVED the costume.

But I had no intention of wearing it.

EVER!

After last night's disaster, just the thought of attending another party actually made me want to... VOMIT!

I guess I'm still traumatised or something.

At this point, I plan to skip the Halloween dance and just help out at Brianna's ballet party. I've already spent the money I was paid, so I'm pretty much STUCK doing that one.

But I'm not going to stress out about it. I mean, what could possibly go wrong at a party for a bunch of six-year-olds?!

I'll be spending the rest of Halloween night sitting on my bed in my pyjamas, staring at the wall and sulking.

Which, for some reason, always makes me feel better ☺.

I just hope Chloe and Zoey don't get mad at me and decide they don't want to hang out with me anymore.

Having friends is SO complicated!

Which, BTW, reminds me that I am NOT looking forward to seeing Brandon in biology class tomorrow.

That look on his face just keeps haunting me.

I feel really awful about acting the way I did, but I couldn't help it.

I'm pretty sure by now he

HATES MY GUTS!!

If I was him, I definitely would. ☹!!

All day MacKenzie and Jessica have been giving me the evil eye and whispering about me.

I'm so sick of them, I could just SCREAM!

Apparently, they're mad at me for that whole chocolate fountain fiasco.

And MacKenzie's spreading the rumour that I only came to her party to try to humiliate her so Brandon wouldn't want to take her to the dance.

This whole thing was THEIR fault!

If Jessica hadn't smacked my plate like that, those little pieces of fruit wouldn't have fallen into the fountain and made it malfunction.

I can't stand MacKenzie, but I'd NEVER try to mess up her birthday party.

I mean, how immature would THAT be?!

Even though I hadn't seen Chloe and Zoey since the party, they must have heard all the gossip.

I wasn't surprised to see they'd left a note on my locker.

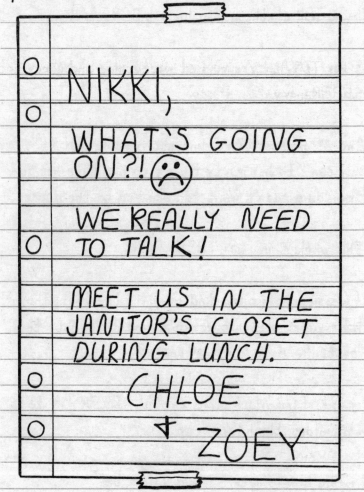

I had no choice but to come clean and give them all the nitty-gritty details about what had happened and why I'd left the party early.

Only, I didn't mention the part about Brandon since I was still confused about all that.

I was TOTALLY surprised when Chloe and Zoey got SUPERangry.

Not at me, but at MacKenzie and Jessica.

They said they'd suspected something bad had happened to me after I left so suddenly without telling them.

They hugged me and said they were really sorry I'd had to go through all that alone.

Of course, that just made me cry.

So Chloe, Zoey and I had a really good group cry.

It was Chloe's idea that the three of us resign from the clean-up crew. And Zoey totally agreed.

They said we were NOT going to tolerate MacKenzie and Jessica's bullying any longer.

I couldn't believe my ears! I knew Chloe and Zoey had their hearts set on attending the dance as the clean-up crew and doing that phony "My date's a band member!" thing.

Unless, of course, Jason or Ryan ask them to go, which they haven't . . . yet.

But they said it was no biggie. And even though the three of us wouldn't be going to the Halloween dance this year, there was always next year.

I could NOT believe that my wonderful BFFs would make such a HUGE sacrifice just for ME!

I got this huge lump in my throat and I wanted to cry all over again.

Zoey composed a letter stating that we were resigning from the clean-up crew and the three of us signed it.

Then we gave the letter to Jessica, since MacKenzie had appointed her as her personal secretary for all official Halloween dance committee correspondence.

At first Jessica just stared at us really mean.

Then she snatched the letter right out of my hand.

"It's about time you wrote MacKenzie an apology letter. The poor girl was traumatised. Now let's just hope she accepts it. If I was her, I sure wouldn't!"

I couldn't believe Jessica actually said that.

When MacKenzie opens our letter, she'll be in for a little surprise. And, of course, she'll probably have a big hissy fit and create a lot of drama.

I'm going to need years of intensive therapy just to recover from having a locker next to that girl.

BTW, today in biology, Brandon barely said hi and then ignored me the entire hour.

I'm guessing that he's mad at me too.

It sometimes feels like the ENTIRE world is mad at me.

WHATEVER!!! ☹!!

Today we started the gymnastics section in gym class.

I think I might actually be allergic to gymnastics, because whenever I get within ten feet of a piece of equipment, I break out in a rash.

Our gym teacher placed Chloe and Zoey in the intermediate group because they were both pretty good.

But I got stuck in the beginner group because she said I needed a lot of work on "fundamental skills".

The first fundamental skill she requested that I master was "not falling off".

Surprisingly, I caught on really fast.

And, with courage and discipline, I had the potential of earning a perfect score of 10. Just like those girls on the Olympic gymnastics team.

ME ON THE BALANCE BEAM, "NOT FALLING OFF".

ME ON THE UNEVEN BARS, "NOT FALLING OFF".

My gym teacher said she was really proud of the progress I had made in class today and gave me a B+.

I now have a renewed respect for gymnasts, especially those who have completely mastered "not falling off".

Since MacKenzie is in our gym class, I was not that

surprised when she came over and told Chloe, Zoey and me that she was having another emergency meeting today.

She said it was to approve the resignations of some committee members and that attendance was mandatory.

We were happy and relieved she had agreed to let us quit. So we skipped lunch again and went to the auditorium.

MacKenzie opened the meeting by saying that all resignations had to be approved by her. And that until that happened, Chloe, Zoey and I were still official members of the clean-up crew.

Then things started to get really WEIRD.

She became very emotional and said, "Due to a recent incident in my life — caused by a person who shall remain nameless — I can no longer serve as chairperson of the dance and I tender my resignation. However, I'll continue to support the dance by attending, *IF* it actually occurs."

Then, as if on cue, ALL the set-up committee members resigned. Then the food committee members. Then the entertainment, publicity and decoration committees.

MacKenzie smiled really big and said, "As chairperson, I officially approve all the resignations, including my own. All ex-committee members are now free to leave."

The other clean-up crew members and I just sat there in shock as every last person got up and walked out.

Except MacKenzie.

"OMG! It looks like I totally forgot to vote on your resignations. Which, BTW, means YOU five are now the Halloween dance committee. If you decide to have it, you better get busy because you have a ton of work to do. And if you decide to cancel it, make sure you notify Principal Winston and the student council. Although, I wouldn't want to be the one to disappoint the entire school like that. Good luck! LOSERS!"

I just sighed and rolled my eyes at her.

"MacKenzie, you are SUCH a drama queen. You can't just resign like this and walk out!"

"Oh yeah?! WATCH ME!!"

Then she cackled like a witch and sashayed out of the auditorium.

I just HATE it when MacKenzie sashays!

By sixth hour, the entire school was gossiping about how MacKenzie and the other committee members had resigned.

Everyone was saying the Halloween dance was going to be either cancelled or a complete DISASTER!

WHY?

Because no one believed that the clean-up crew —
Chloe, Zoey, me, Violet and Theodore, the biggest
DORKS in the entire school — could pull off the
biggest social event of the semester.

And they were absolutely right.

☹!!

I spent the entire night tossing and turning and barely got any sleep.

I also had the most horrible nightmare.

I was at the Halloween party dancing in a chocolate bar costume.

And for some reason, I couldn't feel my toes, feet or legs.

Suddenly, I realised in horror that my body was melting into a pool of warm, gooey chocolate.

And even though I was desperately screaming for help, everyone at the dance just laughed and started dipping pieces of fruit into my melted body parts.

Talk about TRAUMATISING!

Boy, was I ever relieved when I realised it was all just a silly nightmare.

This morning the members of the clean-up crew had an emergency meeting in the library about the Halloween dance.

Only, it really WAS an emergency because we had to decide whether or not to cancel it.

I was in the library writing in my diary and waiting for the others to arrive when Brandon walked in.

I was surprised to see him. Especially since it seemed like he'd been avoiding me the past few days.

Brandon placed a stack of books on the front desk and kind of hesitated like he was a little nervous or something. Then, finally, he walked up to me.

126

"So, um. . . how's the Halloween dance coming?"

"It's NOT. Haven't you heard? MacKenzie quit. And took practically ALL the committee members with her."

"There's still you and a few others, right?"

"Unfortunately, we'll be having a meeting in the next ten minutes to officially cancel it," I said, glancing at the clock. "I'm just waiting for everyone to arrive."

Brandon folded his arms and sighed. "That's too bad. I was looking forward to going."

I had to admit, he DID look a little disappointed. And for some reason, that bothered me.

"Well, I'm sure you and MacKenzie can find something else to do Halloween night. Maybe you guys can go trick-or-treating?"

I threw my head back and did a fake little laugh to try to hide my snarkiness.

"MacKenzie? Who said I was taking MacKenzie?"

"Um. . . everybody!"

"Oh. Well, I guess everybody's wrong, then," Brandon said with a shrug.

I stared at him in disbelief. OMG! Did he just say he WASN'T going with MacKenzie! WHAT?! How could he NOT be going with MacKenzie?

"Well, *somebody* needs to tell her that. She already has your costumes picked out."

Brandon glanced out the library window like our conversation was boring him out of his skull. "I did. She asked me to take her and I said no."

"You told MacKenzie NO?!" I said, trying not to act surprised.

HOW could he say no to MacKenzie? WHY would he say no to MacKenzie? No one EVER says no to MacKenzie!

"She said she'd just cancel the whole thing," Brandon said looking really annoyed.

"Okay, wait a minute! Are you serious? MacKenzie said she'd cancel the dance for the entire school unless you agreed to be her date?"

"Something like that."

"How could she?! That's just totally. . . CRAZY!"

"Yeah, she set you guys up."

I tried to wrap my head around everything I'd just heard.

"Okay. So, MacKenzie resigns, and when the dance gets cancelled, nobody ever finds out she lied about you taking her. And in the end the entire school gets mad at US and not HER! UNBELIEVABLE!"

"If you cancel the dance, she wins," Brandon said matter-of-factly.

"WOW! This is just so. . . WOW!! I don't know how we'd ever pull it off."

Brandon grinned and winked at me. "You'll figure it out. I'm afraid MacKenzie's met her match."

"Listen, bud. Have you seen the clean-up crew?! Actually, YOU should be afraid! Be VERY afraid!!"

We both laughed really hard at my silly little joke. It was kind of strange, but talking to Brandon not only gave me a whole new perspective on things, it also made me feel A LOT better.

Soon we were talking about school and stuff. That went really well until he smiled at me kind of shylike and stared right into my eyes.

Of course I started blushing like crazy.

Then it got so quiet we could hear the library clock ticking.

I think he felt a little embarrassed too, because he

bit his lip and started drumming his fingers on the magazine shelf.

Suddenly he slapped his forehead and gave me this really goofy but cute look.

"Duh! I almost forgot what I came in here for."

"Yeah, me too." I trudged over to the front desk and grabbed his pile of library books to process them back into the system. "It looks like none of these are overdue. So, are you returning—"

Brandon didn't give me a chance to finish. "No, actually, I came in here to ask if you'd go to the dance with me?"

My mouth dropped open and I just stared at him.

I could NOT believe my ears.

"Wait. Did I hear you correctly? You just asked me if—"

"Yeah, I did."

"Oh! Well. . . okay. SURE! I guess," I stammered, blushing more than ever. "IF there is a dance."

I was trying to act nonchalant about the whole thing. But inside my head I was like,

YEESSS ☺!!

"Cool," Brandon said, nodding his head and looking a little relieved. "Very cool. And let me know if I can help you guys out."

"Sure! And thanks! You know. . . for asking me." I was smiling from ear to ear and couldn't stop.

"Hey, no prob. Well, I better get going. See you in bio."

Still a bit dazed, I watched him walk to the door and disappear into the hall.

FINALLY!

Brandon had asked me to the Halloween dance!!!

I was so happy I started doing my Snoopy "happy dance".

La, La, La!
I'M . . .

La, La, La!
SO . . .

La, La, La!
HAPPY!!

Soon Chloe, Zoey, Violet and Theo arrived, and we began our meeting.

When I told them about MacKenzie and why she had bailed on the school dance, they could hardly believe it.

Who would have thunk that girl could be so selfish, devious and manipulative.

Talk about EVIL! MacKenzie makes the Wicked Witch of the West look like Dora the Explorer.

I'm just saying. . . !

By the end of the meeting we had all agreed upon two things.

First, we were NOT going to let MacKenzie get away with her dirty little scheme.

And second, the students of WCD were going to have the best Halloween dance EVER!

Courtesy of the clean-up crew ☺!!

The only thing that bothered me was that I was going to be a little busier than I had anticipated.

I was supposed to be:

1. Helping out at the ballet class Halloween party

2. Working on the dance committee

3. Doing that "My date's a band member!" thingy with Chloe and Zoey

AND

4. Hanging out with Brandon as his official date to the dance!

ALL AT THE SAME TIME!

I've gone from "socially challenged" to "socially chic" in just one day.

But I was pretty sure all the scheduling conflicts would simply work themselves out in the end.

I mean, look at those Hollywood party girls.

Aren't they at every party in every city at the same time all while hanging out with their BFFs and boyfriends?

If they can do it, how HARD can it be?!

And everyone knows those celebutants have a combined IQ lower than an ortho retainer.

The good news is that my days of being a not-so-popular party girl are finally over.

☺!!

Mrs Peach has agreed to let us meet in the library every morning to plan the Halloween dance.

She is such a SWEETHEART!

We had a vote and I got elected chairperson.

Which also means it will be entirely MY fault if the whole thing flops!

Violet is in charge of entertainment. Zoey is in charge of set-up. Chloe is in charge of decorations. Theo is in charge of clean-up.

Everyone wanted me to do publicity so I could make us some really cool posters.

However, we still needed someone to be in charge of food.

And about twenty-four more people to help.

That's when I came up with the brilliant idea to place a new sign-up sheet on the bulletin board right outside the office to try to recruit more volunteers.

Some of the jocks and CCPs are so IMMATURE!

The good news is that we got one new volunteer, Jenny Chen.

I suggested that everyone ask a friend or two to help out since we are superdesperate for people.

Brandon stopped by again to take our official Halloween dance committee picture for the yearbook.

So I guess that means we're official ☺!

After our meeting was over, I planned to surprise

Chloe and Zoey with the exciting news that Brandon asked me to the dance.

I had been dying to tell them since yesterday, but I was waiting for the perfect moment.

I was all set to break the news when we saw their crushes, Jason and Ryan, in the library flirting with two CCP girls.

If Chloe and Zoey had been wondering if those two guys were going to ask them to the dance, they definitely got an answer.

A big fat NO!!

I couldn't believe that Jason and Ryan asked two cheerleaders, Sasha and Taylor, to the dance right in front of Chloe and Zoey like that.

Well, maybe not exactly in front of them since the three of us were kind of spying on them through the bookshelves. But still. . .!!

It was suddenly VERY obvious to me that the two hours Jason and Ryan had spent dancing with Chloe and Zoey at MacKenzie's party meant nothing at all. Those guys had tossed them away like two used pieces of Kleenex and asked CCP girls to the dance.

Chloe and Zoey were heartbroken.

But they said having a supportive BFF like me made it a lot easier to deal with the emotional wretchedness of their failed romances.

After that there was no way I could bring myself to tell them about Brandon and me going to the dance together.

I felt SO sorry for them.

But I've also got my own problems to worry about. I've been so OBSESSED with the Halloween dance that I TOTALLY forgot we were having a geometry test today.

The teacher gave us a complicated problem, and we had exactly forty-five minutes to find X, Y and Z.

At first I just stared at the page and started to panic.

Then I realised I was making the problem way more complicated than it really was.

I must have turned into a math genius or something because suddenly it was like I totally understood what I was supposed to do.

I ended up completing the test in no time at all.

Then I took a short nap while the other slowpokes tried to finish before the time was up.

When everyone was finally done, the teacher collected our tests, graded them and handed them back to us.

I took one look at mine and was absolutely

CONBAFFLELATED!!

Which, BTW, means confused, baffled and frustrated.

That's when I totally lost it and yelled at my teacher, "Excuse me, but what's with all the red ink? It looks like you had a really bad nosebleed and used my geometry test as a tissue or something!"

But I just said that inside my head, so nobody else heard it but me.

Although, I have to admit, my geometry teacher WASN'T the first person to criticise my maths skills.

Last year I signed up to be a maths tutor for the sixth graders.

I was really happy because it paid a whopping $10 per hour.

And if I put in 100,000 hours of tutoring by the end of the school year, I could make enough money to actually become a millionaire!

With that kind of cash, I could buy vital personal necessities like an iPhone, a designer wardrobe, extra art supplies AND a private helicopter to fly me to and from school every day.

I mean, like, how COOL would it be if I actually owned a helicopter?!

Chloe, Zoey and I would have the best carpool in the entire school.

ME picking up Chloe and Zoey for school

ME
dropping off
Chloe and Zoey
after school!

And MacKenzie and the rest of the CCPs would be
SUPERjealous of us.

Anyway, my first week as a maths tutor went really
well. I was going to LOVE my exciting new life as a
self-made millionaire.

ME,
making a
TON of
MONEY!!

Unfortunately, when everyone got their maths
homework back, the complaints started to
pour in.

I felt REALLY horrible about the whole thing.

So I tried to say something really positive that
would help rebuild their shattered self-esteem.

But I don't think my positive outlook on the situation made anyone feel any better.

So I resigned from my tutoring position and refunded all the money I had been paid.

Mainly because it was the right thing to do.

Plus, I'm VERY allergic to angry mobs.

OMG!! I had such a severe reaction, I thought I was going to have to call an ambulance or something.

Thank goodness my geometry teacher drops our lowest test score before she calculates our final maths grade for the term.

But still! If my parents find out I just failed my geometry test, they're going to

KILL ME!!☹!!

FRIDAY, OCTOBER 25

ARRRGGGGGHHH!!

I'm so FURIOUS with MacKenzie Hollister, I could. . .
literally just. . . SPIT!

GGRRRRR!!

Not only did she totally RUIN the chances of the
school having a dance by quitting at the last minute,
but she made sure everything was left in total
CHAOS.

150

I had no idea the situation was so bad until I asked each committee member to present a status report at our meeting this morning.

Zoey went first. She said MacKenzie had arranged for the parents of some of the CCPs to cover the expense of having the dance at the same country club as her birthday party.

However, when Zoey called to find out the set-up time, she was told that our reservation for the dance had been CANCELLED by the previous chairperson.

Since the CCPs were no longer involved with the dance, their parents were no longer paying for it to be held at the country club.

Which meant we didn't have a location for the dance ☹!

That's when I suggested that Zoey ask Principal Winston about using the gym or the cafeteria.

But Zoey said she had already checked.

The cafeteria wasn't available because the Junior League was having a UNICEF fund-raiser and the gym wasn't available because the floor was scheduled to be refinished for basketball season.

"Basically, we don't have a place for the dance. And we don't have any money to PAY for a place for the dance. That's the end of my report. Any questions?" Zoey said, and collapsed into her seat.

Nobody had any questions. Which, BTW, was a good thing, because Zoey was NOT in a very good mood right then.

I thanked Zoey for sharing her very thorough and informative report.

Violet's report for the entertainment committee was next.

She said the band for the dance had also been cancelled by the previous chairperson. The band was no longer available, but their manager was giving us a full refund. In ten days.

"So far I haven't found any bands that are available next week or willing to work for FREE. Which means we don't have any music for the dance."

I thanked Violet for sharing her very thorough and informative report.

It was the same story with decorations and food.

Chloe said that the order for Halloween decorations had been cancelled, and Jenny said the caterer had been cancelled. And both Chloe and Jenny were expecting refunds. AFTER the dance.

Theo added that IF there was a dance, he was definitely willing to clean up after it.

I had my entire reputation on the line as chairperson of the Halloween dance. But, thanks to MacKenzie, we had no location, no band, no decorations and no food.

And to ensure that the dance was a total FLOP, she had arranged it so we wouldn't have a single dime to PAY for a location, a band, decorations or food.

We took a vote and it was a unanimous decision. The Halloween dance was officially

CANCELLED!

It got really sad and quiet in the room and I felt like crying.

And even though all of this WASN'T our fault, I couldn't help but feel like we had let down the entire school.

The worst part was that I was the one stuck with announcing the bad news to the student body.

Which I decided to put off until Monday.

Very soon the black slime mold in the locker room shower was going to be more popular than me.

After school my dad told me to take care of the leaves in the backyard. I was supposed to rake and Brianna was supposed to put them in plastic bags.

I HATE, HATE, HATE

having to do chores with Brianna 😞!!

It took me HOURS to get those leaves into a big
pile and Brianna was no help WHATSOEVER!

Thanks to Brianna, I ended up with leaves, twigs and other crud stuck in my hair. I actually looked like I had a new afro hairstyle or something!

I was so MAD! I wanted to stuff her inside a plastic bag and set her out on the curb to be hauled away with the leaves.

But, of course, you can't do that kind of stuff to your little sister or brother, even when they really deserve it. Plus, it probably won't go over that well with your parents.

WHY, WHY, WHY was I not born an ONLY child???!!!

☹!!

I have a terrible headache and I've been feeling superdepressed all day ☹.

I've pretty much given up on the Halloween dance.

Short of a major miracle, it's NOT going to happen.

Plus, I have more important things to worry about.

Like, for example, my nutty sister, Brianna. Her fairy phobia seems to be growing worse.

I think Mom and Dad should seriously consider getting her into some type of counselling or therapy.

Every single night for the past week Brianna has woken me up to go to the bathroom with her because she's afraid.

The fact that she was waking me up in the middle of the night WASN'T the thing that was really bothering me.

It was HOW she was waking me up that was driving me NUTZ!

I considered myself very lucky that Brianna hadn't POKED my eye out yet.

So I did what any perfectly normal, sleep-deprived, raving MANIAC would do in my situation.

I promised Brianna I'd KILL — I mean, get rid of — the tooth fairy so she could start going to the bathroom by herself. Then I could start sleeping nights again.

So in the wee hours of the morning, Brianna and I snuck downstairs to the kitchen so we could make up a special spray that would keep the tooth fairy away.

NIKKI'S HOMEMADE FAIRY REPELLENT

1 cup bottled spring water

$^3/_4$ cup vinegar

$^1/_2$ cup strained tuna fish oil

$^1/_2$ cup strained sardine oil

1 teaspoon ground garlic

1 teaspoon onion powder

Pour ingredients into bottle and shake vigorously for 1 minute or until mixed. For best results, spray liberally in areas where fairy is not wanted. Will repel fairies and most flying insects for 23 years. Excess can be refrigerated and stored for up to 7 days for use as a zesty vinaigrette salad dressing.

Okay, I admit I just made up the recipe right there on the spot to trick Brianna into believing the fairy repellent would actually work.

I poured the liquid into an empty spray bottle and it actually looked pretty real. The only small problem was that the spray SMELLED a lot like a dead walrus. On a hot summer day. In Phoenix, Arizona.

Brianna was nervous about the whole thing and was afraid the fairy might get mad at us if I sprayed her.

Kind of like that time Dad sprayed those hornet wasps and they chased him around the garden for five minutes until he hid behind some rubbish cans.

It was my brilliant idea for me to wear protective gear. I didn't have a choice but to play along to get Brianna to believe the fairy spray would actually work.

After rummaging through her toy box, Brianna handed me her blue plastic diving mask with a snorkel attached.

She said it would help keep the spray out of my eyes and prevent the fairy from gouging them out if she got, like, REALLY violent.

Although, to be honest, I was more worried about Brianna gouging out my eyes than some fairy.

Then Brianna gave me her toy tennis racket with a broken string to use as a fairy swatter.

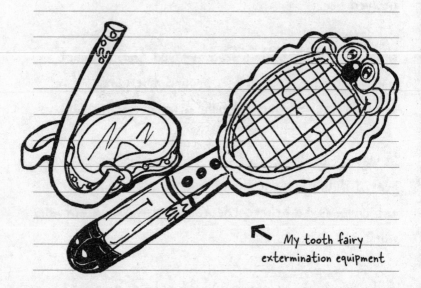

← My tooth fairy extermination equipment

Unfortunately, as soon as I put on the face mask, it started to fog up.

And I was having a hard time breathing through that snorkel.

I felt like the

SPRAY-ER-NATOR!

HASTA LA VISTA, FAIRY!

I sprayed Brianna's bed, desk, lamp and chair with the fairy repellent.

Then I sprayed behind her curtains and inside her toy box.

I was just about to call it a night when Brianna started pulling stuff out from under her bed so I could spray under there.

Then she began tossing junk out of her closet so I could spray in there too.

And she insisted that I spray her Hello Kitty backpack, Barbie CD player and Tickle Me Elmo doll, just to be safe.

I tried to convince Brianna that she had absolutely nothing to worry about.

Because IF the tooth fairy WAS in fact hanging around her room, she was probably totally dripping in stink by now. That poor fairy was going to have to rush back to fairyland and soak in a tub of Mr Bubbles, tomato juice and disinfectant for at least a week.

STINK
FUMES

"OMG!!
WHAT is this
STINKY STUFF?!
It smells like a
DEAD WALRUS!
I'm outta here!"

TOOTH
FAIRY

But Brianna started whining really loud and saying we needed to spray her sock and underwear drawer.

I was like, "Shhhh! You better quiet down before you wake up Mom and Dad! Or we'll BOTH be in big trouble!!"

Soon the spray bottle started making gurgling sounds because it was empty.

I was trying to get out the last few drops when
suddenly the doorknob clicked and the bedroom door
sloooowly opened.

Brianna and I both stared at the door and then each other.

I was like, What the. . . ??!!

"Oh, no! It's the F-F-FAIRY!" Brianna stuttered in horror.

Then she dived into her closet and slammed the door behind her.

Unfortunately, it wasn't the fairy.

I almost wish it had been.

Instead, it was . . .

MOM and DAD!!☹

And I could tell that they were NOT happy.

But what really weirded me out was that my dad's right eye started twitching.

I guessed that it was probably because the room reeked of sardines, tuna fish and vinegar.

Okay. I could understand why my parents might have been a little upset.

It was 2:00 a.m. and we had just totally trashed Brianna's room.

And sprayed enough repellent to fumigate two small, very smelly, fly-infested pig farms.

That's when it occurred to me that, just maybe, I had taken the whole fairy prank thing a bit too far.

To make matters worse, I think the spray was starting to make me feel light-headed and dizzy.

Or maybe I was suffering from oxygen deprivation due to breathing through that snorkel for fifteen continuous minutes.

I thought about hiding the bottle of fairy repellent

171

and the toy tennis racket behind my back and trying to act natural.

As natural as I could considering the fact that I was in my pyjamas wearing a blue plastic diving mask with a snorkel.

My parents were still just standing there with shocked looks on their faces.

Unfortunately, that snorkel thingy made my voice and breathing sound just like Darth Vader's.

But with a really wicked lisp.

"Hi, Dag! Hi, Mog! *Cheee-whoooo.* Whath up! I'm willy berry thorry I woke you up. *Cheee-whoooo.* I wuz justh working on my scieneth project and Brianna's room got a bit methy. *Cheee-whoooo.* LUKE, I AM YOUR FATHER!! *Cheee-whoooo.*"

Lucky for me, Mom and Dad laughed at my joke.

Then I explained that I was just testing out a

new homemade insect repellent/vinaigrette salad dressing/air freshener called Sardine Summer Splash.

And that it was an extra-credit homework assignment.

For gym class.

And extra credit is a good thing!

When Brianna came crawling out of the closet, I knew I was dead meat. I was going be grounded forever if she spilled about my little prank.

But she totally backed me up and told Mom and Dad she had helped me make a special spray to get rid of a little pest in her bedroom.

Thank goodness she didn't tell them the pest was the tooth fairy!

My parents just assumed it was a bug or something and believed the whole story.

I just hope Brianna has finally got over her fairy phobia.

One thing is for sure. . .

It'll be really nice to start sleeping again without having to worry about waking up to find one of my eyeballs lying on my pillow looking at me.

EWWW!

HOW GROSS WOULD *THAT* BE!!

It's the wee hours of the morning and I'm so exhausted I can hardly keep my eyes open.

Mrs Hargrove stopped by this evening to drop off the face-painting supplies for the ballet class Halloween party next Thursday.

She also gave me a rubbish bag that contained a "supercute costume".

She said her niece bought it especially for me to wear to the party and they just knew the kids were going to love it.

That's when I started to get this really bad feeling about Mrs Hargrove's niece.

I was like, "Oh, by the way, I don't think you ever told me your niece's name. Since she goes to WCD, I probably know her."

"Actually, she's one of your good friends. MacKenzie

Hollister! She said you guys have lockers right next to each other and you came to her birthday party last week."

"MacKenzie?!" I gulped.

For a split second it felt like I was going to lose the meat loaf I had eaten for dinner.

"Um. . . yeah. I guess you could say MacKenzie and I are really good . . . locker neighbours."

I vaguely remembered overhearing MacKenzie mention an aunt Clarissa back in September.

My head was spinning as I thanked Mrs Hargrove and trudged upstairs to my room.

WHY in the world had MacKenzie told her aunt I was the best artist in the school?!

Especially after she had compared my artwork to poodle vomit.

And WHY had she suggested that I paint faces for the ballet class Halloween party?!

One thing was VERY clear to me. I smelled a RAT! A really big, stinky RAT!!

LITERALLY.

Inside the bag was the most hideous-looking rat costume I had ever seen in my life.

And it totally reeked of sweaty armpits, stale pizza and disinfectant spray.

I almost gagged.

I guessed that the costume was probably the mascot for some popular restaurant for kids. But it smelled so bad that customers had complained and the manager had thrown it away.

Then, after it had been buried in a Dumpster full

of rubbish for weeks, some high school kid found it and sold it on eBay for $3 to fund his iTunes addiction.

MacKenzie bought it and then gave it to her aunt to give to ME!

Sometimes I wonder if I'm the only person at my school who believes Satan's kid sister has a locker right next to mine.

Anyway, I started feeling really sorry for myself.

While most students in our city would be attending their school's Halloween dance, I was going to be stuck at the Westchester Petting Zoo wearing a stank rat costume and entertaining a bunch of bratty little ballerinas.

How DEPRESSING! I felt like crying just thinking about it.

While everyone else was having fun, I'd be having a BOO-HOO at the ZOO!! ☹!!

My life was so PATHETIC it made me want to—

Suddenly the craziest idea popped into my head!

I tried really hard to ignore it, hoping it would just crawl back into the deep recesses of my brain or wherever crazy ideas come from.

Then I thought, Why not? What do I have to lose?

I rushed over to my computer, went online and did a search for local Halloween haunted houses.

Lucky for me, the place I was interested in was open on Sundays until 7:00 p.m.

I called and spoke with the manager of the facility and explained my situation. He was in complete agreement with my plan as long as we secured permission from Principal Winston.

Since the future of our dance was in limbo, I placed the guy on hold and called Principal Winston's home number, hoping that the three of us could speak together in a conference call.

I started by apologising profusely for disturbing Principal Winston at his home on a Sunday evening and explained that I had an urgent matter to discuss.

However, it took me a while to convince him that I wasn't a prank caller and that the manager of a haunted house really needed to speak with him ASAP regarding a school function.

Within ten minutes all the details had been hammered out and Principal Winston gave me permission to move forward with my plan.

I was ecstatic and started doing my Snoopy "happy dance". AGAIN!!

La, La, La!
I'M . . .

La, La, La!
SO . . .

La, La, La!
HAPPY!!

Next I e-mailed everyone on the dance committee:

HI EVERYONE,
MEET ME IN THE LIBRARY ON
MONDAY AT 7:00 A.M.
FOR AN EMERGENCY MEETING!!
AND BE READY TO ROCK ☺!!
NIKKI

Then I ran downstairs and raided the refrigerator.

I'm pulling an all-nighter and need every ounce of energy I can get my hands on to stay awake.

WHY?

Because the WCD Halloween dance is back on with a vengeance!

Due to the pure GENIUS of one very FIERCE chairperson.

Namely. . . ME! ☺

My new idea for our Halloween dance is totally

KA-RAY-ZEE!

But in a really good way.

OMG! It's almost 6:00 a.m. and our meeting is in one hour.

Gotta go shower and eat breakfast. . . !

!!

I didn't get any sleep last night, so I'm superexhausted. But I'm also deliriously HAPPY ☺!!

BOO!!
(AT THE ZOO)

WCD Middle School
Annual Halloween Dance

Thursday, October 31st
7:30 p.m. to 11:00 p.m.

A Most Frightening Experience at the

WESTCHESTER ZOO
HALLOWEEN HAUNTED HOUSE

We've plastered the ENTIRE school with our posters and flyers!

And now everyone is buzzing about the dance. Which, BTW, is being held on the premises of the biggest haunted house in the city, sponsored annually by the Westchester Zoo.

I've heard "Boo at the ZOO" a million times already and it's not even third hour yet.

There are so many students wanting to help out that I had to put up another volunteer sign-up sheet and then add a second page.

Our meeting this morning went really well and turned into a big brainstorming session. And by the time it was over, thirty-nine people had shown up.

Zoey reported that the Westchester Zoo was happy to host our dance at no charge and set-up was going to be from 3:00 to 6:00 p.m. on Thursday, October 31.

Chloe reported that the art classes were making an assortment of Halloween decorations for extra credit. And the maths club was donating two dozen pumpkins they planned to carve using equilateral, isosceles and scalene triangles.

Violet reported that she still hadn't found a band that would play for free. But since she had an iTunes collection of 7,427 songs, she could throw together a playlist and be our resident DJ.

Theo added that he and a few members of the jazz band had started a group and were willing to do a forty-five-minute set for free, just for the experience of performing before a live audience.

Jenny said that the home-ec classes had agreed to bake chocolate chip cookies and cupcakes. And she had arranged for the owners of Pizza Palace to donate punch, pizzas and assorted flavours of wing-dings with dipping sauces.

Then the science club members volunteered to help with both set-up and clean-up.

I could NOT believe everything for the dance had fallen right into place like that!

Although, I still hadn't made up my mind about my Halloween costume.

Chloe and Zoey had made it very clear that they hated my bag of trash idea. So I decided to wear Mom's Juliet costume.

Zoey says she is going to be Beyoncé, since she looks a lot like her. She's going to wear an outfit from Beyoncé's latest video and sign autographs at the dance.

ZOEY

CHLOE

Chloe says she wants to be the character Sasha Silver from her favourite book series, *Canterwood Crest*. It's about these frenemies at a private riding academy and it's kind of like

The Clique, but on horseback. Chloe plans to wear fancy riding gear with boots.

And Brandon says he's going to be one of the Three Musketeers. How COOL is THAT?! I can't wait to see him.

Now that I think about it, I'm really glad we're not doing my bag of rubbish costume idea.

I'd be totally embarrassed to have Brandon see me wearing something so immature and silly.

BTW, I still haven't told Chloe and Zoey yet that Brandon asked me to go to the dance.

I was going to tell them last week, but when the dance got cancelled, I figured, why bother?

Although, to be honest, I'd rather just keep it a secret for now.

I guess I'm really worried Brandon is going to change his mind for some reason.

And then I'll be so HUMILIATED I'll have to transfer to a new school or something.

But I know I have to tell Chloe and Zoey sooner or later.

Definitely. . . LATER!

Now that the Halloween dance is back on again, I don't think I'm going to have time to go trick-or-treating with Brianna this year.

I'm kind of bummed out because I've done Halloween ever since I was a little kid and it's always been such a blast!

Except for that one year when Chucky Reynolds, the neighbourhood bully, started snatching kids' trick-or-treat bags.

He stole MY sweets too! However, instead of getting mad, I decided to get even. And I waited until the next Halloween to do it.

Our neighbour had a vegetable garden and I noticed there were like a zillion worms in her compost pile. So I knocked on her door and asked her really politely if I could borrow two cups of worms. She looked at me like I was crazy, but she said yes.

Needless to say, I ran into Chucky on Halloween night. And when he demanded that I hand over my treats, I was actually kind of happy about it.

Chucky the Bully   ME

My little trick worked perfectly and Chucky Reynolds NEVER snatched another kid's sweets again! ☺!!

AAAAAHHHHH!!

Okay. THAT was me screaming!

WHY?

Because I can't believe the HORRIBLE MESS I've got myself into!

AAAAAHHHHH!!

That was me screaming AGAIN!

My situation is BAD! VERY BAD!!

Right before lunch I got a note from
Chloe and Zoey to meet them in the janitor's
closet.

They said they couldn't wait to show me their new
Halloween costumes.

But more than anything, I thought this would be
the PERFECT time to FINALLY tell them about
Brandon asking me to the dance.

Since he hadn't cancelled on me (yet, anyway!) and
the dance was in only two days, I thought now would
be a good time to tell my BFFs.

So this was the plan I had inside my head. . .

After I got done raving about Zoey's Beyoncé
costume and Chloe's Canterwood Crest riding
costume, I was going to tell them about MY
fabulous Juliet costume. And maybe even invite
them over to see it after school today.

Then I was going to blurt out:

GUESS WHAT?!
BRANDON ASKED
ME TO
THE DANCE!!

Chloe and Zoey were going to be so surprised that they'd start screaming and jumping up and down.

We'd end the little celebration with a group hug.

I was also pretty sure that during the dance, Chloe and Zoey would insist that I secretly meet them somewhere to give them all the juicy details.

Which meant I'd probably have to tell Brandon I

needed to go to the bathroom, like, once every hour. Just to update my BFFs.

THAT was the PERFECT plan I had inside my head.

But unfortunately, things didn't happen the way I had planned.

When I got to the janitor's closet, I told Chloe and Zoey that I had some surprising news for them too.

They said, "Okay! You first!"

And then I said, "No! You first!"

Then they said, "Come on! YOU go first!"

And then I said, "No way! YOU go first!"

So they finally said, "Okay! We'll go first."

Then they made me close my eyes.

"SURPRISE!! Here's OUR costumes!!"

When I opened my eyes, I was expecting to see a Beyoncé outfit and a riding outfit.

But instead, I saw THREE rubbish bag costumes!!

The exact same rubbish bag costume I had suggested two weeks ago that Chloe and Zoey had called really LAME!

"Aren't they CUTE?!" Chloe said, smiling really big and giving me jazz hands.

"Do you NOT love them?!" Zoey giggled.

"We figured that since the three of us were going to be hanging out at the dance together. . ." Chloe started.

"We might as well hang out as three BAGS OF RUBBISH!" Zoey finished.

"OMG! OMG! You—you guys SHOULDN'T have!" I stammered.

Only, I really meant it.

"Well, since you had your heart set on us being bags of rubbish, we didn't want to let you down. Especially after you agreed to do that clean-up crew thing with us. And if it wasn't for you, we wouldn't even be having a dance," Chloe said, tearing up a little.

"Yeah, we were being a little selfish about the whole costume thing. So after school yesterday, we met at Chloe's and worked on them until midnight. It's the least we can do to show you how much we appreciate having a really great BFF like you!" Zoey said, dabbing her eyes.

"Yeah, one who'll stick by us through thick and thin, no matter what!" Chloe added.

Then Chloe and Zoey both grabbed me and we did a group hug.

Then they said, "Okay. Now what did YOU want to tell US?!"

I just stood there looking at Chloe and Zoey and feeling REALLY horrible!

I couldn't believe they were actually giving up their cool costumes.

To dress up like LAME bags of rubbish?!

JUST FOR ME??!!

I didn't deserve great friends like Chloe and Zoey!

But another part of me felt bad because I knew true friendship was supposed to be based on honesty.

Which meant I had no choice but to tell them the truth. . .

That Brandon had asked me to the dance and I had accepted.

That I planned to mostly hang out with him all night. Not them.

That I was going to be a beautiful, romantic and moody Juliet. NOT a bag of rubbish.

So I just blurted it out.

"I'm really sorry, Chloe and Zoey, but I CAN'T wear

that bag of rubbish costume or hang out with you guys at the dance!"

At first they were confused and kind of stunned.

"What do you mean. . . ?" Zoey sputtered.

"I d-d-don't understand. . . !" Chloe stuttered.

Then, as it sank in, their confusion turned into hurt and they both just stared at me.

Okay, I liked Brandon a lot, and I really, really wanted to go to the dance with him.

But there was NO WAY I could do this to my two best friends.

So I smiled really big and gave them jazz hands to lighten the mood.

"Um. . . what I actually meant was. . . I can't wear that costume or hang out with you guys. . . UNLESS we get yellow rubber gloves, crazy wigs and sunglasses!! We gotta have those! Right?"

Chloe and Zoey looked totally relieved and smiled at me.

"OMG! You almost gave us a heart attack!" Chloe chuckled.

"Rubber gloves, wigs and sunglasses, coming right up!" Zoey said. She opened a bag and tossed one of each to me.

"Great! Then I guess we're ready to ROCK!" I said, smiling.

Even though deep inside I was so frustrated I felt more like crying.

"We're going to have SO much fun!!" Zoey squealed.

"I can hardly wait!!" Chloe giggled.

So that's why I'm now in my bedroom screaming.

AAAAAHHHHH!!

Mainly because Thursday evening could turn into a major DISASTER.

I'm supposed to wear a rat costume and hang out with the ballerina brats.

I'm supposed to wear a Juliet costume and hang out with Brandon.

AND I'm supposed to wear a bag of rubbish costume and hang out with Chloe and Zoey!

All at the same time!

How did I ever get myself into this MESS?!

Okay, here's an idea. . .

I'll just call Brandon, Chloe, Zoey and Mrs Hargrove and tell them I'll be home sick Thursday evening with a bad case of BUBONIC PLAGUE.

AAAAAHHHHH!!
😞!!

This morning at breakfast I was

TOTALLY GROSSED OUT!!

I think I've lost my appetite for the rest of the year.

My mom put my dad on a diet last week and he has started doing midnight raids on the refrigerator. It's very obvious because he forgets to put stuff back in the fridge.

Unfortunately, I always know at breakfast when he's had cookies and milk the night before.

Hey, call me a picky eater! But, personally,
I don't like my Fruity Pebbles with sour milk
chunks.

If this keeps up, I think I'll need to have a little talk with Mom about this situation.

I'll remind her that marriage is based on mutual love, trust and respect, and that she didn't marry Dad for his looks.

But, most important of all, I'll gently bring up the fact that Dad gaining a few extra pounds won't really matter when I DIE OF STARVATION because all the food in the house is SPOILED!

I'm just saying. . . !!

Anyway, right now I'm feeling like the most HORRIBLE person on earth ☹!

I can't believe I'm LYING to my friends like this!

Well, if not exactly lying, I'm NOT telling them important stuff they should probably know.

I haven't told Brandon, Chloe or Zoey that I'm

supposed to be helping out at the ballet class party during the dance.

I haven't told Chloe and Zoey I'm supposed to be Brandon's date to the dance.

And I haven't told Brandon I'm supposed to be hanging out with Chloe and Zoey all night as bags of rubbish.

WHY?

Because I'm trying really hard to make everyone HAPPY.

The last thing I want is for Brandon, Chloe or Zoey to be disappointed in me as a friend.

But if I tell them the truth, all three of them will probably HATE me!

Unless I secretly try to. . . ??

NO WAY!!

It will NEVER work!!

Besides, I'm NOT a lying, sneaky little RAT, like
MacKenzie!

Or am I...?!

☹!!

Okay, this is probably the longest diary entry in the entire history of the world.

But that's because tonight was

UNBELIEVABLE!

Thank goodness we don't have school on Friday due to parent-teacher conferences. I'm TOTALLY EXHAUSTED and barely have enough energy to write this!

Brianna's ballet class party started at 7:00 p.m. at the petting zoo.

Lucky for me, it was only one building over from the zoo's haunted house, which was where we were having our Boo at the Zoo dance.

Mom dropped me off fifteen minutes early so I could change into my rat costume.

The eyeholes must have been made for a taller
person, because I was too short to see out of them.

The best I could do was peek through one of the rat's enormous nostrils.

All I had to do was paint some faces and lead a few games and then I was OUTTA THERE!

Most of the girls in the ballet class were wearing cute little animal costumes because of the petting zoo theme.

My sister, Brianna, was the Easter Bunny. Actually, a PSYCHOPATHIC Easter Bunny.

She gathered all the other kids around her and then yelled at the top of her lungs, "Hi, there! I'm the real, live Easter Bunny! Since you all have been good little girls, would you each like a GIGANTIC CHOCOLATE BUNNY?!!"

Of course everyone got really excited and shouted, "YEEESSSSS!"

I could NOT believe what Brianna said next!

It's pretty obvious that my kid sister has some SERIOUS issues!

She didn't have the slightest idea I was Mr Rat and I decided not to tell her.

Hanging out with the girls and painting their faces was actually kind of fun.

A unicorn told me everything she wanted for Christmas, like I was Santa Claus or somebody.

And this cute little witch whispered into my huge rat ear that if I came to her house in the middle of the night and bit off all her brother's toes, she would keep it a secret!

Just in case I wanted to do something like that.

And I felt really bad because I think I may have traumatised this cute little cat.

She pointed at me and shrieked, "I'm scared! That big kangaroo is stinky and has eyes inside his nose!!"

I was like, AMEN, SISTER!!

After I finished painting faces, I led several rounds of the Hokey Pokey dance. It must have been 120 degrees inside that costume.

I was relieved when Mrs Hargrove asked the girls to be seated for pizza and punch.

I decided to sneak away for a while and told

Mrs Hargrove I was going to take a short toilet break.

I grabbed my duffel bag and raced back to the bathroom.

It felt good to finally get out of that smelly rat getup.

I splashed cold water on my face and arms to cool down and freshen up.

But my heart was pounding from the excitement of what I was about to try to pull off.

Within minutes I had completely changed into my Juliet costume.

I pinned on the wig thingy, smoothed on three layers of Very Berry Krazy Kiss lip gloss and then gazed at my reflection in the mirror.

It took a few seconds for me to get over the shock of what I saw.

I barely recognised myself!

I threw my duffel bag over my shoulder and hurried down to the haunted house, which was located in the zoo's community centre.

Once inside, I found the nearest bathroom and hung my bag on the hook behind the door of the very last stall.

I put on my mask, walked back down the hall and stepped inside the dance.

Even though it had just started, the room was already packed with people. The decorations and food we had brought in looked fabulous!

And the whole haunted house scene with the antique furniture, cobwebs, and assorted animated witches, ghosts and ghouls that randomly popped out of coffins and closets really helped set the fun mood.

Even though I was Juliet, I felt more like Cinderella because everyone around me was staring.

Most of the CCP girls just glared and whispered.

The crazy thing was that nobody seemed to recognise me. And I wasn't that worried about Chloe and Zoey because they were up front helping Violet with the music.

Violet was onstage rocking the house with some hot tunes by Justin Bieber! I think she was supposed to be an evil clown or something, but I couldn't really tell.

That girl is TOO weird. But in a good way.

I couldn't wait to see Brandon. When I finally spotted him, I couldn't help but stare.

OMG! He looked SO handsome in his costume. I thought I was going to faint!

I think he was really surprised
by my costume too because
he blinked a few times and
then just stared right back
at me.

We just stood there kind
of staring at each other
for what seemed like
forever.

It wasn't until I
said, "Hi, Brandon,"
that he finally
seemed sure it
was actually me.

He brushed his hair
out of his eyes, smiled
and offered me a seat.

"Wow! Nikki, you look, I
mean, your costume is
really. . . cool."

"Thanks, Brandon. I think you make a great Mouseketeer!"

"Um. . . it's 'Musketeer.'"

"Oh, sorry! Musketeer."

"So. . . would you like to dance?"

"Sure!"

Thank goodness it was a fast song.

Brandon was actually a pretty good dancer. And he was cracking jokes the entire time, which made me laugh really hard.

We were having so much fun I didn't want the song to end.

We were just about to sit down again when I saw Chloe and Zoey heading in our direction.

I was like, UH-OH!

"Brandon, I think I'm going to go to the bathroom and then check on a few things, okay?"

"Sure. I'll be waiting right here."

"Would you like me to bring you anything back? Like some. . . wing-dings?"

"Wing-dings. Um, sounds. . . interesting!

"You're gonna love 'em! Back in a few minutes!"

I headed for the door.

And I got there just in time.

When I peeked back inside, I saw Chloe and Zoey talking to Brandon. Then he pointed in my direction.

I took off running like a maniac down the hall to the bathroom.

I slammed the stall door shut and frantically pulled off the dress and wig and stuffed them into my duffel bag.

Then I slipped into the rubbish bag costume and tied the drawstrings into a bow at my neck.

My fingers nervously fumbled as I put on the hot pink wig, sunglasses and rubber gloves.

Finally.

FINISHED!!

And not a second too soon. Just as I was coming out of the stall, Chloe and Zoey rushed in.

"Hi, Nikki! We've been waiting on you. Brandon told us you were in here. Isn't this great?" Chloe said breathlessly.

"I'm so happy we decided to go with your costume idea! We look SO cute!" Zoey gushed, posing in the mirror.

"Hey, girlfriends! It's time for us to take out the rubbish!" I teased.

We did a quick group hug and rushed into the dance.

Just about everyone was out on the floor having fun. Even the teachers.

I totally avoided the side of the room where Brandon was sitting and prayed he couldn't see me because of the crowd and dim lights.

Although, even if he had, there was no way he would have recognised me. He was not expecting to see me in a wacky rubbish bag costume, and the wig and sunglasses practically covered my entire face.

Chloe, Zoey and I had a blast dancing!

But I was starting to get a little worried about being away from the ballet party for too long.

"Um, guys, I ran into Brandon a few minutes ago and convinced him to try some of our yummy punch and wing-dings. I was going to take him some snacks, but I just found out I have to go drop off papers at the zoo office. Could one of you take Brandon over some punch and a plate of wing-dings and let him know I had to run an errand?"

"Sure!" Chloe said, and headed off towards the food table.

"Hey! I'll come with you," Zoey said, following me out into the hall.

I started to panic.

"NO!! Zoey, you can't!" I almost screamed
at her.

She froze and just kind of stared at me, wondering
why I was freaking out like that.

I plastered a fake smile on my face and tried to
regain my composure.

"Actually, what I meant was, um. . . no, you
CAN'T miss this really great party! I'll be back
in a sec, 'kay?"

Zoey shrugged and smiled. "Sure!"

As soon as she was out of sight, I sprinted back to
the bathroom.

I dived into the last stall, changed back into that
funky-smelling rat costume and hightailed it back to
the ballet party.

I was superworried because I had taken a heck of a
long toilet break.

But it was perfect timing because the girls were just finishing up their dessert of Steaming Witches' Brew Ice Cream Punch and Worms-'n'-Mud chocolate cupcakes.

"Oh, there you are!"

Mrs Hargrove rushed over and tried to peer in at me through the rat's left nostril.

"I think we're ready for another game," she said.

I gave her the thumbs-up sign.

But in my head I was like, WHEW!!

We played Simon Says and Duck, Duck, Goose! and the kids loved it.

Soon Ranger Roger arrived to take the kids around to see the animals.

Since the kids were going to be distracted for the next half hour, I told Mrs Hargrove that the rat costume had got a little warm and I was going to step outside for a few minutes to cool down.

I grabbed my duffel bag, raced to the bathroom and changed back into my Juliet costume.

Within three minutes I was back at the Halloween dance sitting next to Brandon.

"Hey! You're back." His smile could have lit up the entire room.

"Sorry. I just had a few errands to take care of! I'm, like, the most horrible date!"

"No, I don't mind, really. I figured you were going to be kind of busy tonight."

"Thanks for understanding."

Then it got really quiet and I just kind of stared at him with this stupid smile on my face.

I started to get butterflies in my stomach.

That's when I decided to say something witty and intelligent.

"Soooo. . . how did you like those wing-dings?"

"Actually, they were pretty good."

"I just knew you would like them!"

"Oh, I was supposed to let Chloe and Zoey know when you got back. I think I'll just text message them. . ."

"Um, you know what?! Boy, am I hungry! I think I'm going to run over and get us both some more wing-dings. 'Kay? Be right back!"

"Hey, wait! I'll go with—"

But I disappeared before he finished his sentence.

Chloe and Zoey had made their way back to Brandon's table by the time I reached the door.

I raced back to my bathroom stall to change again.

Okay, rubbish bag, rubber gloves, sunglasses and. . . rat head!

NOPE! Wrong party!

Hot pink wig was what I needed.

I tried to calm down.

But knowing that Chloe and Zoey could pop into the bathroom at any second looking for me made me a nervous wreck.

I was back in my rubbish bag costume and at the food table getting more wing-dings when Chloe and Zoey caught up with me again.

"Hi, Nikki! There you are!"

"Brandon said you went to get more wing-dings."

"Yeah! They're delish!!" I said. "So, where do you guys want to sit?"

"Brandon said we could sit with him. There's plenty of room at his table."

"SIT TOGETHER?!" I gasped. "Sure. Umm. . . you two go right ahead. I have to, um. . . go to the. . . bathroom. So I'll meet you guys at the table. 'Kay!"

Suddenly I remembered Brandon's snacks. There was no way I could let him see me in my trash bag costume, so I asked Chloe and Zoey for help.

Umm. . . could you guys give Brandon this little plate of wing-dings for me?

Then I took off running as fast as I could.

ARGH! There was NO WAY I could sit with all three of them.

What was I going to do?!

But my bigger headache was that I had barely two minutes to get back to the ballet party.

I ran to the bathroom stall, changed back into the rat costume and rushed over to the petting zoo.

Ranger Roger was finishing up just as I arrived.

Mrs Hargrove handed me a box of goody bags and peered at me through the rat's right nostril. "As soon as you give these out to the girls, you'll be done," she said, smiling.

I was like, YES!!

I could not believe my crazy scheme was actually working.

Since the ballet party was almost over, parents were lining up at the front door to pick up their kids.

I decided to close out the party in a dramatic way.

"Well goodbye, kiddies! I hope you all had fun with

Mr Rat! I'm on my way to Disney World to visit my cousin Mickey! Bye, bye!"

All of the kids waved goodbye, and a few of them even looked a little sad to see me go.

Just a few minutes more and the whole funky rat fiasco would be history.

I was heading towards the back door when Brianna yelled, "Hey, wait, Mr Rat! Can I come with you?"

"Yeah! I wanna come too!" said the little girl who had tried to convince me to come to her house and chew off her brother's toes.

Pretty soon the whole group of kids was crowding around and begging to come with me.

"I'm really sorry. Maybe next time, okay?"

I turned around to leave but suddenly realised there was a slight complication—

—Courtesy of my bratty sister, Brianna. I couldn't believe this was actually happening to me!

"I'm not gonna let go of your tail until you promise to take us with you!" Brianna screamed.

I had to think fast!

The rat costume was starting to give me an itchy rash and Brianna would not let go of my tail.

I was sure Chloe, Zoey and Brandon were wondering what had happened to me.

"Okay, I have an idea! Everyone close your eyes and make a wish. Then count to ten. And when you open your eyes, you'll all have a wonderful wish to take home with you! Okay!"

All the girls jumped up and down and cheered together. "YEAHHH!!"

"Hey, Mr Rat! I'm gonna wish that I can go to Disney World with you to visit your cousin Mickey!" Brianna said stubbornly.

I was like, Sheeeeesh! Brianna, just let it go, will you?!

"Now let's all close our eyes and start counting. One, two. . ."

All the girls closed their eyes and counted with me.

"Three, four. . ."

I grabbed my duffel bag and flung it over my shoulder.

"Five, six. . ."

I opened the back door. . .

"Seven, eight. . ." And ran for my life!

And I didn't stop running until I had made it safely
back to the dance.

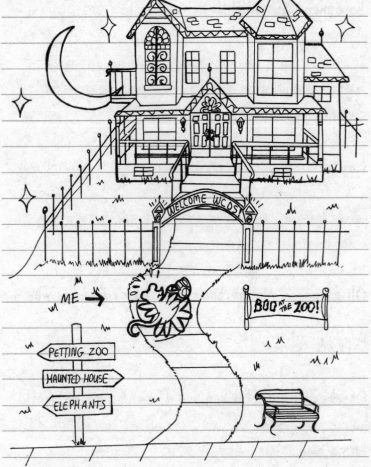

I felt really guilty having to ditch the ballet class like that, but I didn't have a choice.

Although I meant well, all the deception and running back and forth was exhausting.

The dance was going to be over in less than two hours and I planned to enjoy every minute of it.

That's when I decided to ditch the costumes and just have fun hanging out with Zoey, Chloe, and Brandon as plain ol'. . . ME!

All I had to do was change out of the rat costume and into my favourite jeans and sweater.

But as soon as I entered the girls' bathroom, I realised one major obstacle was standing in my way.

MACKENZIE HOLLISTER!

She was dressed as a very chic vampire and was at the mirror applying an extra-thick layer of Bloody Mary Really Scary Red lip gloss.

I thought I was going to have a heart attack right there on the spot.

But mostly I was shocked and surprised she had the nerve to even show up at the dance after trying to undermine the whole thing.

MacKenzie was capable of doing anything to anybody to get what she wanted.

And I was pretty sure she'd do everything within her power to totally RUIN this night for me.

I desperately needed to change my clothes and this was the only girls' bathroom in the entire building.

So I decided to just play it cool by pretending I had to use the bathroom.

I was praying she wouldn't recognise my costume — or rather, HER costume, seeing as she was the one who bought it.

I had just grabbed the stall door handle when suddenly MacKenzie whipped around and stared at me.

I instinctively froze. Then, pretending I wasn't me, I nodded my head kind of friendlylike and waved at her.

Her pouty lips turned into a scowl as she narrowed her eyes at me.

I broke into a sweat.

"EWWWW! What's that horrible smell?!"

I didn't dare say a word for fear she might recognise my voice.

So I just sniffed under each of my armpits and frantically fanned the air under each like, P–U!

Then I held my arms out to my sides and shrugged my shoulders as if to say, Sorry 'bout that!

She rolled her eyes at me, turned back to the mirror and continued applying her lip gloss.

THANK GOODNESS! I wasn't sure if my little antics had totally annoyed or totally disgusted MacKenzie. But I was really happy they had worked!

I quickly entered the stall, dropped my duffel bag on the floor, slammed the door shut, locked it and collapsed with relief against the wall.

WHEW! That was close.

Although, to be honest, I found it a little puzzling that MacKenzie didn't recognise the raunchy odour or the dirty, matted rat fur.

I took off the rat head and dropped it on the floor. I couldn't wait to slip off the hot, scratchy costume and then take it home and burn it in our fireplace.

My comfortable jeans, sweater and sneakers were going to feel like heaven.

Suddenly I heard quick footsteps approach my stall.

Before I knew what was happening, a manicured hand wearing Ravishing Red Revenge sparkly nail polish reached right under my door and snatched my duffel bag.

I frantically lunged after the strap and pulled with all my might. But somehow I must have stepped on that stupid rat head or something.

I slipped, lost my balance, fell over backwards and hit the back of my head on the bathroom floor.

OOOWWWWWW!!!!! I moaned. The ceiling above me was spinning like a merry-go-round. I closed my eyes.

I pulled myself up and massaged the back of my head. The pain was quickly subsiding and luckily I didn't feel a lump or anything.

I staggered to my feet, fumbled with the door lock and peeked out.

Just as I had feared, the duffel bag containing all my clothing and personal belongings had completely disappeared.

Along with MacKenzie.

I was sure she hadn't got very far. And if I went charging out into the hallway, I might even catch her.

But I was a little worried that tackling a fellow student at a school function might end up on my permanent record and negatively impact me getting admitted into a major university after graduation.

Hey, you can never be too careful. I hear some colleges are really picky about that kind of stuff.

I could NOT believe all of this was actually happening to me. I was so frustrated I wanted to scream, but I didn't.

MacKenzie had just stolen my clothes and I was stuck in a bathroom stall wearing a stinky rat costume at the WCD Halloween dance after my secret crush, Brandon, had FINALLY asked me to go.

I was like, PLEASE, PLEASE, PLEASE let all of this just be another really bad dream. I wanted to wake up in my comfy bed wearing my heart pj's and think, WOW! *THAT* was the craziest nightmare EVER!

Only, I didn't wake up. Which meant all of this was real ☹!

So, like any normal girl in my situation, I had a massive panic attack right there on the spot. My stomach started to churn and my knees felt weak.

I kept thinking, *If only* I had bought a new phone instead of that stupid dress for MacKenzie's party. Then I could call my mom and have her bring me some clothes.

Finally, I closed my eyes and took three very deep, calming breaths because I really needed it.

Then I sat down on the toilet seat to focus all my energy into coming up with a solution to my problem.

The problem being, of course, that I really, really needed to get my bag from MacKenzie.

And I had two choices.

I could go the dance in my underwear. Or I could wear the rat costume.

It was a very difficult decision, indeed.

But I decided to go with the rat costume mainly because it offered one important advantage.

When the entire WCD student body witnessed a foul-smelling, mangy rat. . .

1. CHASE DOWN MACKENZIE. . .

My clothes

2. SNATCH A DUFFEL BAG FROM HER. . .

3. AND THEN CHOKE HER UNTIL SHE TURNED
BLUE IN THE FACE AND PASSED OUT. . .

THEY'D HAVE NO IDEA IT WAS ACTUALLY
ME. ☺!!

So I put on the rat head and rushed back into the
dance.

As I entered, two seventh graders dressed as
Klingons stared at me and gasped.

"P-U! What is THAT smell?!"

"I don't know, dude! But whatever it is it just
burned out all my nose hairs."

I just waved at them both kind of friendlylike.

I squeezed through the crowd and found a spot along the front wall. From there I scanned the entire room trying to locate either MacKenzie or my duffel bag.

I should have known exactly where to find her!

She was sitting next to Brandon, twirling her hair and trying to flirt with him. And he was looking superbored and trying his best to ignore her. All the while probably wondering where the HECK I was.

Poor guy!

HALLELUJAH! I spotted my duffel bag in an empty chair right next to MacKenzie!

I slowly crept over to the long row of tables they were sitting at. And when it appeared that no one was looking, I quickly dove underneath.

It was supergross crawling around under there, but I was very, very desperate to get my duffel bag back.

MacKenzie was so distracted with Brandon that nabbing it was actually a piece of cake. I probably could have stolen the dress she was wearing and she wouldn't have noticed.

I was just superHAPPY to have my bag back!

In a matter of minutes I'd be sitting right next to Brandon, gazing into his dreamy eyes and having fun with Chloe and Zoey.

Or maybe NOT!

As I approached the door, there was a huge commotion.

Most of the students at the dance were crowded in a half circle staring at something. I couldn't tell what.

Everyone was laughing and pointing, and before long the music stopped and the house lights came on.

Since I was chairperson of the dance and it was my personal business to know what was going on, I pushed my way through the crowd to take a look.

I immediately wished that I HADN'T.

"Hey, look, everybody! There's Mr Rat! We found him!" Brianna screamed gleefully, and pointed at me!

Within seconds I was mobbed by the entire ballet class and they started hugging me.

I had a heart attack right there on the spot!

I could NOT believe those little brats had followed me to the dance.

Principal Winston and a few chaperones stood nearby looking very worried.

I was sure they were trying to figure out where all the little kids had come from and what they were doing at a middle school dance.

I walked up to Principal Winston and peeked at him through my left nostril.

"Um, Principal Winston, I know you're wondering what's going on here and I can explain every—"

But that was as far as I got because that's when Mrs Hargrove, my mom and dad and the parents of the other little girls came rushing into the dance.

And they were NOT happy.

It got really loud and confusing because the parents were really upset and demanding to know why Principal Winston had allowed their six-year-olds into a middle school party.

And, of course, Principal Winston was upset and demanding to know why the parents had let their six-year-olds crash his middle school party.

Finally, Principal Winston asked Violet to pass him the microphone.

"Okay, everyone, please quiet down. It looks like all the children are safe and accounted for. But can anyone explain how they got here?"

That's when MacKenzie raised her hand.

Principal Winston motioned for her to come forwards and handed her the microphone. But before she said anything, she put on a fresh layer of lip gloss.

OMG! That girl is SO vain!

"Hello, everyone. I know what happened, and I personally feel it is my duty to make sure everyone knows the truth. . ."

Deep down, I was a little relieved that MacKenzie was going to explain everything so I wouldn't have to.

"It's all HER fault! The RAT! Right there!" MacKenzie snarled and pointed at me.

Everyone in the entire room immediately turned and stared at me. Although I felt SUPERembarrassed, at least no one knew who I was.

I never would have thought I'd be happy to be wearing that rat head.

That's when MacKenzie walked over and snatched it right off my head.

"It's NIKKI MAXWELL's fault! And I think she owes us all an explanation for why she endangered the lives of these poor, innocent children and RUINED our Halloween dance!"

I was so HUMILIATED I wanted to DIE! Plus, it felt like I had a really bad case of hat hair.

Then MacKenzie shoved the microphone into my hand, sashayed over to Principal Winston, folded her arms, and glared at me with this little smirk on her face.

I didn't know what to say or where to begin.

It didn't help that Chloe, Zoey and Brandon had somehow made their way to the front of the crowd.

They were standing a few feet away with these confused looks on their faces, whispering to one another.

I stared at the floor and sighed. It was so quiet in the room you could hear a pin drop.

Principal Winston cleared his throat. "Well, Miss Maxwell, we're waiting. . . ?!"

"Um. . . actually, I had agreed to help out at the ballet class Halloween party, BEFORE I was voted chairperson of the WCD party. I was just trying to do them both at the same time. Which, in hindsight, maybe wasn't such a good idea. Anyway, the girls must have followed me over here. I'm really, really sorry for messing things up. . . !"

When I looked around the room, everyone was just staring at me — Principal Winston, kids from school, teachers, parents, the ballet class and even my family.

I felt really HORRIBLE for having ruined everything for ALL these people!!!

I handed the microphone back to Principal Winston and turned and rushed out of the dance.

I didn't know where I was going, but I had to get out of there.

Chloe and Zoey caught up with me in the hall.

"Wait, Nikki. What's going on?!" Chloe asked.

"Yeah! What are you doing in that rat getup? And where is your trash bag costume?!" Zoey added.

But before I could answer, Brandon walked up.

"I was wondering where you were. Why did you change out of your Juliet costume?"

Chloe and Zoey looked at Brandon and then they both narrowed their eyes at me.

"Juliet costume?! What Juliet costume? You were wearing a Juliet costume?!" Chloe sputtered.

"But where's your rubbish bag costume?!" Zoey asked, still confused.

I just stared at the floor and didn't say anything.

"Wait a minute!" Chloe said, folding her arms and

glaring at me. "You've been running around all night in three different costumes?! Why are you trying to trick us?"

"If you didn't want to hang out with us tonight, you could have just told us," Zoey said, obviously hurt.

Brandon must have felt sorry for me or something because he came to my defence. "This is all my fault. I asked her to the dance. I didn't know she was supposed to be hanging out with you guys."

Shocked, Chloe and Zoey spun around and both shouted at me. "BRANDON ASKED YOU TO THE DANCE?!!!"

I could NOT believe the mess I had made. "Listen, guys," I muttered, "all I can say is that I'm sorry. Really, really sorry!"

I faced Chloe and Zoey. "I didn't have the heart to tell you about Brandon asking me to the dance after what happened with Jason and Ryan. I knew how important this dance was for you. I just

REALLY wanted to be there for you guys. . ."

Then I turned to Brandon. "So, maybe I should have told you I couldn't go to the dance because I was going to be too busy. I planned to help out with the ballet class party AND hang out with Chloe and Zoey. But I figured I could just try to do it ALL. But now I see that wasn't fair to you."

Chloe, Zoey and Brandon just looked at me and didn't say anything.

I didn't blame them for being angry with me. I was angry at myself.

I was the worst friend EVER!

With tears streaming down my face, I turned and ran down the hall and right out the front door.

Once outside the building, the first thing I did was throw the rat head into some bushes.

I really HATED that thing!

I found a park bench about thirty metres away and flopped down on it in utter despair.

I stared up at the full moon. Other than the faint sound of the zoo animals and the rustling of leaves in the trees, it was a quiet night.

It felt good being outside in the cool night air, even though I felt really bad inside.

It seemed no matter how hard I tried to make something work, it always turned out to be a complete disaster.

I was SUCH a loser ☹!

I sniffed and wiped away my tears.

"Mind if I sit down?"

I thought I was alone, so hearing a voice startled me.

I was surprised to see Brandon standing right behind me. He sat down next to me on the bench.

"I just needed to get some fresh air," I said, trying to pretend like I had not been crying. "I'm REALLY sorry for ruining everything. . ."

"What? Nothing was ruined."

"Yeah, right! Just our date. And the dance. And the kids' Halloween party. . ."

"Actually, hanging out with you tonight has been. . . well, 'exciting' is a really good word."

"Sure, about as exciting as getting a cavity filled."

"Come on! We weren't even HAVING a dance until you took over. Right?"

"Yeah, I guess so."

"And those little kids liked you so much they followed you over here."

"Well, if you put it that way. . ."

"Anyway, I mainly came out here to give you a really important message."

Like I needed any more bad news. I had already ruined two parties in one evening.

I got this huge lump in my throat and felt like I was going to cry again.

"Yeah, I was kind of expecting that. From Principal Winston?" I asked sadly.

"Nope."

"My parents? I'm probably grounded until my eighteenth birthday."

"Nope. A friend."

"I still have friends? After all this, I'm sure Chloe and Zoey wouldn't want to be seen with me." I sniffed and wiped a tear.

"A very special friend. He's here waiting to talk to you."

"Where?!" I spun around, peering into the darkness around me. "I don't see anyone."

"Close your eyes and I'll ask him to come out."

"What?!"

"Come on! Just close your eyes. He's a little shy."

I closed my eyes.

"Hey, no peeking!"

"I'm NOT!" I stopped peeking.

"Okay, now open them."

I opened my eyes and couldn't help but crack up laughing.

Then he did a really awful Mickey Mouse impersonation in this silly high-pitched voice. "Excuse me, I'm looking for a rat friend of mine. Have you seen her around here?" He couldn't help chuckling at his own stupid joke.

I played along.

"Actually, I haven't seen her. Sorry!"

"Well, I kinda like her. She's nice. And I just wanted to hang out with her some more. Can you tell her that? If you see her?"

"Sure!" I said, giggling uncontrollably. "If I see her, I'll tell her."

"Thanks."

"No prob!"

We both laughed so hard it hurt.

Brandon had a really wicked sense of humour. And nothing seemed to faze him at all.

I really liked that about him.

He took off the rat head and handed it to me.

"I think this thing belongs to you."

"Unfortunately, it does." I took it from him and shoved it under my arm.

"Can I ask you a really personal question?" he asked.

Brandon's mood suddenly seemed to have changed and he was gazing at me superserious.

I hesitated for a moment. I had no idea what he was going to ask me.

"Yeah. Sure."

"WHY does this thing smell so bad? WHEW!" He scrunched up his nose and narrowed his eyes like they were stinging from the odour.

We cracked up laughing again.

Brandon and I walked back to the building and Chloe and Zoey met us at the door.

They both looked a little upset and I just knew they were going to tell me off. I really deserved it.

"Nikki, why didn't you tell us when Brandon asked you to the dance?" Chloe said.

"Yeah. We could have helped out with the ballet party so you could have been at the dance the entire time!" Zoey added.

"We're your BFFs. I can't believe you didn't let us help you," Chloe said, looking at me kind of sadly.

I got a lump in my throat and felt like crying again. I couldn't believe they were actually upset because I hadn't let them help me.

"You're right. I should have told you both. I guess I didn't want to burden you with all my problems."

"Nikki, have you lost your mind?! That is just about the STUPIDEST thing I've ever heard you say!"

"Yeah! You must be suffering from oxygen

deprivation or something from wearing that rat head, because you are a talking like a CRAZY person!" Zoey added.

I could NOT believe they said that to me. Chloe and Zoey are the best friends EVER!!

They both came up to me and gave me a big hug.

"We forgive you. But if you EVER do something like this again, we'll personally force you to listen to a Jessica Simpson CD," Chloe said.

"For two whole hours!" Zoey added.

"I think the punishment is a little extreme. But I promise, I'll never do this again!" I giggled.

"By the way, those little girls really LOVE you!" Chloe gushed. "They said they want Mr Rat to come to their party next year too!"

"And guess what! Chloe has come up with the coolest

little keepsake for them to remember you by," Zoey said excitedly.

"Actually, I got the idea from my new book, *The Secret Life of a Teenage Party Planner*," Chloe explained, "but I'm going to need Brandon and Zoey to help out."

I thought it was a really cute and creative idea too. It took a lot of patience, but Brandon managed to take a very special picture with Chloe's new BlackBerry, while Zoey went around collecting e-mail addresses for each of the ballet girls' families.

Then, thanks to Chloe's superquick fingers, by the time everyone arrived home they all had a special little surprise waiting in their e-mail inboxes.

I'm sure the girls loved it.

Brandon is such an AWESOME photographer ☺!

Even though there were still technically ninety-two minutes left, everyone pretty much assumed the dance was over.

We were all just waiting around for the official announcement.

Principal Winston met with the chaperones for a few minutes and then walked over and whispered something to Violet.

Violet nodded to Principal Winston and picked up the microphone. "May I have your attention. I have an announcement to make on behalf of Principal Winston. He says he's aware that our dance is technically not over yet. However, he has asked that I inform you all that due to the unexpected disruption, effective immediately, we need to. . .

GET THIS PAR-TAY STARTED!!!"

Anyway, the second half of the Halloween dance was even more fun than the first half.

I almost freaked out when MacKenzie came up and told me the Halloween dance totally rocked. She said I had done a really great job as chairperson. Of course, she took partial credit for the success and insisted that I thank her publicly because none of it would have happened if she hadn't resigned.

Sometimes I think her severe lip gloss addiction has damaged her brain cells. That girl is so incredibly VAIN!

Then, when I asked MacKenzie if she had a date for the dance, she totally LIED about it.

She started bragging that her date was actually the lead singer of the band that was about to come onstage. And since he was going to be busy the rest of the night, she was hanging out with her BFF, Jessica. Whose date, BTW, was ALSO in the band.

I was really shocked to learn that two respected

CCP girls like MacKenzie and Jessica were using the old "My date's a band member!" trick.

How pathetic was THAT?!

Anyway, the lead singer, Theodore L. Swagmire III, was REALLY happy to hear THAT bit of news. Especially since he'd wanted to ask MacKenzie but was pretty sure she was going to say no.

When Brandon asked me to dance during a slow song, I thought I was going to DIE!

It was so TOTALLY romantic!!

OMG! My stomach had so many butterflies I thought I was going to have to grab MacKenzie's cute little $600 Dolce & Gabbana purse and use it as a barf bag.

But the biggest surprise of the night was that Brandon and I were voted Cutest Couple. . . by my BFFs, Chloe and Zoey!

Which was kind of weird because at this point we're just friends and still getting to know each other.

It's not like we're a "REAL" couple yet.

At least, I don't think so.

Unless HE thinks we are but I don't know it.

But I'm pretty sure he DOESN'T.

Unless I'm WRONG!

OMG!! What if I'm RIGHT?

What if he really likes me and thinks we're a couple?

Only, I don't know it YET!

Wait a minute. . .

I'd be the FIRST person to know it!

Wouldn't I?

DUH. . . !!

I'M SUCH A DORK ☺!!

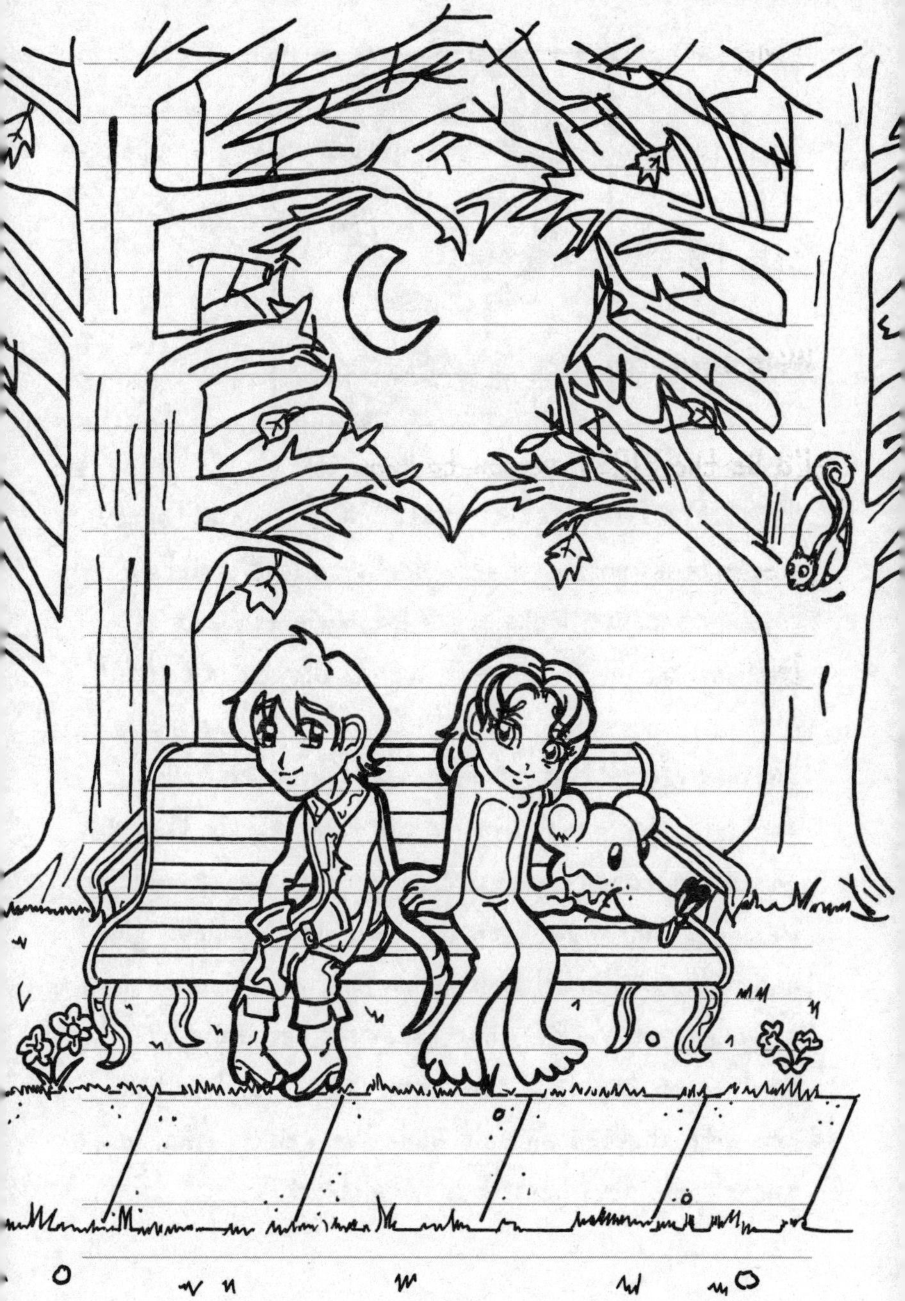

Rachel Renée Russell is an attorney
who prefers writing tween books to legal briefs.
(Mainly because books are a lot more fun and
pyjamas and bunny slippers aren't allowed in court.)

She has raised two daughters and lived to tell
about it. Her hobbies include growing purple flowers
and doing totally useless crafts (like, for example,
making a microwave oven out of Popsicle sticks, glue
and glitter). Rachel lives in northern Virginia with
a spoiled pet Yorkie who terrorises her daily by
climbing on top of a computer cabinet and pelting
her with stuffed animals while she writes. And, yes,
Rachel considers herself a total Dork.